Anton Chekhov

THE WOMAN IN THE CASE

AND OTHER STORIES

translated by
April FitzLyon and Kyril Zinovieff
and with an introduction by
Andrew G. Colin, LL.B., PH.D.

LONDON
SPEARMAN & CALDER

'The Woman in the Case'
was first published in 1953 by
Neville Spearman Limited and
John Calder Limited
10 Fitzroy Street
London W.1
It was copyright in 1953 by
April FitzLyon and Kyril Zinovieff
and was printed in Great Britain by
Page Bros. (Norwich) Ltd.
in 11 on 12 pt. Baskerville

CONTENTS

INTRODUCTION

I HAVE been asked to write an introduction to the twenty-three stories by Anton Chekhov translated by April Fitz-Lyon and Kyril Zinovieff, under the title *The Woman in the Case, and Other Stories.*

The appearance of these short stories, unpublished in English till now, is, to my mind, a literary event which will be commented upon on both sides of the Atlantic.

I recently attended a literary luncheon in Scotland. My neighbour was a well-known English writer. When I spoke to him of Anton Chekhov as 'the famous Russian author' he reproved me without a trace of a smile on his face. 'What do you mean by "Russian" author? Chekhov has by now become an English writer.' Thinking about that remark, I am now inclined not to disagree entirely with that eminent English author. Anton Chekhov is much appreciated in the English-speaking world and his renown is ever increasing. Russian literature is fairly well known to the Western public at present, and it can be said that Russian classical fiction and drama are as much the property of the English-speaking people nowadays as is Russian music. The English author was therefore not far from the truth.

However, full justice has not yet been done to Chekhov. Not all of his short stories have yet been translated into English. The present book, therefore, should be warmly welcomed. The work has been done by an excellent team. It is a genuine and artistic translation from Chekhov's Russian originals.

One of the reasons why I accepted the invitation to write a preface to this book is the fact that Chekhov means a great deal to me. Years ago I went to Taganrog (in South Russia) and saw the house in which he was born. I recently went to Badenweiler, in Southern Germany, to visit the house in which he died. I saw the hotel room in which he breathed his last. I went out on the balcony and listened to the stirring of the firs and pines around the house. It was midnight. The scenery remotely, yet distinctly, brought to mind Chekhov's own story: *The Lady With The Dog*, one of the most poignant stories in the Russian language; particularly the scene where Anna Sergeyevna and her lover were sitting in Oreanda, in the Crimea.

> '. . . They were looking down on the sea and were silent. Yalta was barely visible through the early morning mist. Motionless white clouds had settled on the mountain peaks. Leaves did not stir on the trees, grasshoppers were chirruping, and the monotonous, dull sound of the sea, coming from down yonder, spoke of rest, of the eternal sleep which awaits us. The same murmur rose from below before Yalta or Oreanda were in existence, the same murmur goes up now, and shall go up, just as indifferent and dull, when we shall be no more. . . .'

This description came back to me on that night as I looked at the scene of Chekhov's last few days. The firs and pines stirred exactly as they had done when the author listened to them from his sick bed.

Almost fifty years have passed since he died at the age of forty-four. He might have been with us still.

What would he have given to Russia and to the rest of the world had he lived his full span? No one can tell; but his genius was noticeably gaining in depth and in universal appeal towards the last five years of his brief adult life.

I have been brought up on Russian writers among whom Chekhov took a very prominent place. I know his background and the actual settings of most of his stories and plays. I am one of the very few men still alive whose contact with Chekhov has been direct. When a small boy, I was told that

the tall bespectacled gentleman standing in the entrance hall
of the mansion where we lived in St. Petersburg was Chekhov,
the writer. True, the short contact was merely a symbol.
Everything that took me nearer to Anton Chekhov was
subsequent to that symbolic encounter. But it had been real
and will remain unforgettable.

To revert to this book. As I said before, the twenty-three
stories selected by the translators have not been translated
into English till now and, if some of them have, none to my
knowledge have been published. Another important fact
is that out of the twenty-three stories appearing in this
volume twenty were written by Chekhov between January,
1884, and June, 1887, that is, within three years and five
months. This is a short period, compared with the whole of
his active literary career which comprised twenty-five years
—from 1879 to 1904.

Let us consider the first of these two important points.
Everyone knows that most of Chekhov's short stories and all
his plays have been translated into English for some con-
siderable time now. The distinguished Englishwoman,
Constance Garnett, assisted by her husband, has rendered a
great service to the English-speaking people on all the five
Continents by translating very faithfully the majority of
Chekhov's short stories.

But she has not translated all of them. Even if she had, it
would not have prevented someone else from doing the same,
just as a variety of translators have, at various times, under-
taken to translate Shakespeare into Russian. As it happens,
Constance Garnett's translations from Chekhov into English
have been followed (with varying results) by others, such as
Kotelyansky, Marion Fell, etc.

However, none of the stories selected by April FitzLyon
and Kyril Zinovieff in this book are to be found in the
thirteen volumes of Constance Garnett's translated Chekhov
stories.

Why? I can only make surmises as to the various reasons.

The bulk of Constance Garnett's work was done between 1910 and 1923. I believe it is true that most of Chekhov's stories which had not been included by him in his list of stories to be republished were simply inaccessible to translators abroad. These stories had all been published in Russian periodicals. Yet, they could not easily be found, even in Russia, let alone in England or the United States.

Of course, with the appearance of Chekhov's complete works in 1944–51 (*Works by A. P. Chekhov, 20 volumes,* published in Moscow) such stories came to light. They took their place in the chronological order of Chekhov's work and are available to everyone who is able to read Russian.

Thus, what Constance Garnett was unable to do during her lifetime, April FitzLyon and Kyril Zinovieff were fortunately in a position to do just now.

A few remarks concerning the second important factor relating to the stories in this volume: the period in which they were written. Chekhov wrote most of them when he was between twenty-four and twenty-seven years old and when his life centred in or around Moscow. The few stories in this selection written in the first half of 1884 belong to the period when Chekhov was reading for his final examinations in medicine at Moscow University. All the rest was penned when he had become a qualified physician. Nevertheless, the period was so short that we may speak of this book as a selection of 'young Chekhov's' stories, with the exception of three.

Let me deal with the twenty early stories first.

To be sure, Chekhov was far from a beginner in 1884. He started as a very young man and in 1884 had reached the position of an author whose stories are invariably published immediately on completion.

By 1884 he had nothing in his briefcase; on the contrary, he had to write fast so as to deliver his new short stories in time for publication.

It would, however, be a grave error to assume that it was

the same Chekhov who wrote all these stories. In 1884 he had just started on the road of emancipation from the part of an amusing and carefree beachcomber. He had already begun to treat his work very seriously. In 1884 we still find a number of jolly miniatures some of which are (let us admit it) not of any literary value, in the Chekhovian sense of values. They are short pieces, hastily written 'to order' and, most probably, accepted only because they were by Anton Chekhov. We do not find anything like it in the stories of this book which belong to 1885, but we find Chekhov returning on four occasions to this sort of miniature in 1886 and 1887.

However, the gradual dropping of insignificant writing by Chekhov does not meant the shedding of his humour. On the contrary, the stories in this book, dated 1885, are the most typical for Chekhov's youthful humour.

Thus we already have two groups based on the twenty early stories appearing in this volume: the gay trifles written mainly in 1884 and the truly humorous and better stories belonging to 1885. I should add two more groups: the psychological one and that which must be classed as tragic. The psychological stories show us the way which Chekhov was resolved to travel. They had already put in their appearance in 1884, although they were then clad in comical garb. This, however, could only mislead the very unsophisticated. Such stories can also be found under 1886. The last main group, the tragic one, is, characteristically enough, peculiar to 1885 and 1886, with an emphasis on the latter year. Gaiety, if not humour, was already leaving Chekhov for good at that period. His development strangely echoed that of his elder, Nicolas Gogol. Both had started with rollicking laughter and both had died rather young, with all the mirth gone from them, after it had made room, in both cases, for unredeemable tragedy, inseparable from Russian life, as they felt.

Is it not typical that the absolute turning point in

Chekhov's literary career, the point at which he ceased to be amusing and became a very serious writer of undisputed greatness, was the publishing of his longer story *The Steppe*, in 1887? This story, no doubt intentionally, starts not unlike Gogol's *Taras Bulba* and contains descriptions of South Russian places which would pass as coming from Gogol's pen. Yet, no one in his senses would affirm that Chekhov's style was an imitation of Gogol's.

One gets the impression when reading *The Steppe* that Chekhov had made a decision: 'Enough of this merrymaking! Let me try and write something that would be as good as that which Gogol wrote fifty years before me.' And surely, it *was* as good. . . .

This tendency is certainly noticeable in the later stories appearing in this selection, because it began to take shape as far back as 1884.

For the reader's information I shall group the twenty-three stories, irrespective of the order in which they appear in this volume:

A. THE AMUSING TRIFLES
    1. 75,000 (1884)
    2. The Reporter's Dream (1884)
    3. Out of Sheer Boredom (1886)
    4. A Disagreeable Experience (1887)

B. THE HUMOROUS STORIES
    5. The Diplomat (1885)
    6. The Guest (1885)
    7. Mutual Superiority (1885)
    8. The Woman in the Case (1886)
    9. The Eve of the Trial (1886)

C. THE PSYCHOLOGICAL PIECES
    10. Appropriate Measures (1884)
    11. His First Appearance (1886)
    12. The Mask (1884)
    13. Holy Simplicity (1885)
    14. The Lodger (1886)
    15. Sinister Night (1886)

I must warn the reader that the above grouping is entirely of my own making and is not binding upon anyone.

Just a few words concerning the three stories in this book which were written by Chekhov after 1887.

They clearly show how far the writer had travelled on his road to scepticism and to an attitude of mind akin to despair. In *An Unpleasant Incident* Chekhov paints upon a background of a conflict, a psychological portrait of a typical representative of the intelligentsia. The story is painful to read, so true to Russian life of Chekhov's day are the men and women in it, in their utter futility.

In *History of a Business Enterprise* we find a satire which is so camouflaged that it is at first imperceptible. The doings of certain 'progressive' people and their worship of radical luminaries, according to fashion, are shown in a very subtle, yet trenchant manner. So is their return to earth, accompanied by a general lowering of behaviour.

Finally, there is the tragic *A Visit to Friends*. Not tragic in the accepted sense, but in the frame of Chekhov's tragicalness. There are no murders, no suicides, there is not even illness or dire poverty in the story, but there is spiritual murder and spiritual suicide in plenty. The story, which precedes the creation of *The Three Sisters* by only two years and of *The Cherry Orchard* by four, can be understood as a forerunner of these two dramas which Chekhov, for some unexplained reason, wanted to be treated as comedies.

He had no such desire when penning *A Visit to Friends*.

The story is likely to have cost Chekhov very dearly; it must have done. After writing it, he only wrote twelve more and then stopped. It makes one think that he could not go any further. The last stage on Chekhov's road in his search of a solution of the ominous problems of Russian life seems to have been reached in *A Visit to Friends*. The reader, even if not Russian, must be, cannot help to be, moved by this tale of utter frustration.

When we take a close look at Chekhov's *craft*, as it transpires from the stories in this selection, we notice that the master is already fully established in his domain. Gone are the cheaper and cruder effects of the very early years. Chekhov, by 1884, was a powerful writer of short stories, to which I ought to add that he was also the first writer in Russia specialising in short stories on a large scale. Some historians of Russian literature may object and quote Leskov and Garshin. I would not be convinced if they did. I have a good deal of genuine respect for both these writers, but they are not typical short-story writers. Leskov was a novelist, whereas Chekhov never became one. Garshin was, to a great extent, an autobiographer, and this field of writing was not Chekhov's whose forte was usually life around himself, not in himself.

Certain masterly strokes, typical of Chekhov's later work, had already found their way into those early pieces which appear in *The Woman in the Case, and Other Stories*.

When you begin to read a short story by Chekhov, written in the period 1884–1886, you notice at once that you cannot foretell the end. When you come to the end, you must admire the ending, that is, the seal he put on his narrative.

The varying manners of expression of the different classes and callings are brilliantly portrayed even in these early stories. That which had been exaggerated or unnecessarily 'localised', Chekhov himself corrected for later editions of his work. Thus, the emphasis on the uneducated merchant's faulty Russian in *The Mask* was afterwards softened down by the author when he realised that to be humorous did not mean to be crude.

Chekhov's fine understanding of the Russian woman, his sincere sympathy for her lot, his conviction that woman, in the spiritual sense, is higher than man—are all in evidence even in these early stories of his.

There is an interesting item in *The Dream (A Christmas Story)*. We find on page 102 this passage:

> A loud, shrill twang suddenly and unexpectedly resounded above my head, but lasted no more than a second. Something cracked and gave a loud whine, as if in great pain.

This musical motif, in this instance brief and unexpected, is only the first of a long series of interludes of sound in Chekhov's stories and, particularly, in his plays. It must have been calculated to create an uncanny or even an eery atmosphere. This device achieves its aim in the case of the short stories and is quite irresistible in the plays. There we have one particular tune which is always sad, and it reverberates when the play is over. . . .

In *The Sea Gull* it is Dr. Dorn's singing. Ominous music is also encountered in *Ivanov*, in *Uncle Vanya*, in *The Three Sisters*. In *The Cherry Orchard* it is, quite apart from Epikhodov's guitar playing, a mysterious sound coming repeatedly from a distance, and reminiscent of a string which suddenly bursts.

This is very telling. In 1902, when *The Cherry Orchard* was being written, Chekhov reverted, probably quite unconsciously, to the same artistic device which he used back in 1885, in *The Dream*.

Looking from another angle, his imagery had reached a high level, even at the time when the early stories were written.

I shall not quote many examples, but I should like to take these two, from *The Eve of the Trial* (1886):

. . . The feeling experienced by the trigger when the gun misfires. Or:
. . . Not merely frost, but the whole of the Arctic Ocean ran down my back. . . .

One of the attractions of this story, however, is the absence of any conclusion. Another writer, with less artistry, would have given an ending to the story and would have spoilt it. But even at the age of twenty-six, Chekhov would not be likely to lower his already very high standards by a literary *faux pas*.

Before I finish this introduction, I feel compelled to quote and then to refute an assertion by the well-known critic and contemporary of Chekhov, Alexander Izmaylov. He said soon after Chekhov's death: 'Abroad, Chekhov will always remain a translation. Neither those autumnal feelings in the bloom of youth nor this melancholy inspired by the forest, the steppe, the sands, are known to the foreigner's soul. Chekhov's handling of this aspect of the Russian soul is more significant, more lasting than the circumstance that he set a seal, historically speaking, to the nineties and foretold the revolution.'*

I must disagree with him. To the Russians, the English-speaking people are, of course, foreigners. Yet, 'autumnal feelings in the bloom of youth' are known to the Anglo-Saxon race, even if I concede that such emotions may not have been so noticeable in Western Europe at the threshold of the century. On the other hand, melancholy is not a prerogative of the Russian.

I firmly believe that Chekhov's finest shades of feeling, his subtle and sorrow-tinged impressionism are very well understood or at least felt by present-day readers in the English-speaking world.

I shall agree with this: not in every land can Chekhov's beauty and greatness be fully appreciated. That is why his unknown work is not being translated into *all* languages.

* He meant the "pre-revolution" of 1905.

But at least some of his untranslated work is now coming out in an English version, as the present book proves, and this is a more eloquent refutation of Izmaylov's statement than anything I may say.

Izmaylov mentions something else, however, in another connection:

'The chief key to the understanding of Chekhov's moral character lies in his rare truthfulness. I know of no other writer who is so close to the truth and so abhors the slightest hint of falsehood.'

Also, elsewhere:

'For his influence, for the greatness of his powers, unparallelled by any other writer of his epoch, he by right stands first after the creator of *War and Peace*.

There Izmaylov is absolutely right. Chekhov's nobility of mind is, to me, an axiom. His greatness, as a writer, is beyond discussion.

I say that it is very fortunate for anyone to be able to render something by Anton Chekhov which is still unknown to English-speaking readers.

ANDREW G. COLIN
Lecturer in Russian,
Royal Naval College,
Greenwich.

October, 1953.

ACKNOWLEDGEMENT

The translators wish to express their thanks for the great help and advice given by Dr. Colin, whose knowledge of Chekhov's works and of the period has proved invaluable.

THE WOMAN IN THE CASE

SMYCHKOV, a musician, was walking from town to Prince Bibulov's country villa where, to celebrate an engagement, there was to be an evening of music and dancing. On his back lay an enormous double-bass in a leather case. Smychkov was walking along the bank of a river, the cool water of which was running if not majestically, at least extremely romantically.

Shall I have a bathe? he thought.

Without further ado he undressed and plunged his body in the cool current. It was a gorgeous evening. Smychkov's romantic soul was beginning to harmonise with its surroundings. But what a blissful feeling seized his heart when, after swimming along about a hundred paces, he saw a beautiful girl sitting on the steep bank, fishing. He held his breath, overwhelmed by a welter of mixed feelings: reminiscences of childhood, nostalgia for the past, awakening love. . . . Good heavens, and he had thought that he could no longer love! After he had lost faith in humanity (his wife, whom he had loved passionately, had run away with his friend Sobakin, the bassoon-player), his heart had been filled with a feeling of emptiness, and he had become a misanthrope.

What is life? He had asked himself the question more than once. What do we live for? Life is a myth, a dream . . . ventriloquy. . . .

But standing before the sleeping beauty (it was not difficult to observe that she was asleep), suddenly, regardless of his will, he felt in his breast something resembling love. . . . He stood before her for a long time, devouring her with his eyes.

But that's enough . . ., he thought, letting out a deep sigh. Farewell, lovely vision! It's time I went to His Highness's ball. . . .

He looked once more at the beauty, and was just about to swim back, when an idea flashed through his mind.

I must leave her something to remember me by! he thought. I'll hitch something on to her line. It'll be a surprise from 'person unknown'.

Smychkov swam quietly to the bank, picked a large bunch of field and water flowers and, tying it up with a bit of pigweed, he hitched it on to the hook.

The bouquet fell to the bottom, and took the pretty float down with it.

Prudence, the laws of nature, and my hero's social position demand that the romance should end at this precise point, but—alas! an author's fate is inexorable: owing to circumstances beyond the author's control the romance did not end with a bouquet. In spite of common sense and the nature of things, the poor and humble double-bass player was to play an important part in the life of the rich and noble beauty.

When he swam to the bank, Smychkov was thunderstruck: he could not see his clothes. They had been stolen. . . . While he had been admiring the beauty, some unknown rascals had carried off everything except the double-bass and his top hat.

'Damnation,' exclaimed Smychkov. 'Oh men, you generation of vipers! I don't so much resent being deprived of my clothes—for clothes decay—as the thought that I shall have to go stark naked and thus violate social morality.'

He sat down on the double-bass case and tried to find a way out of his awful predicament.

I can't go to Prince Bibulov's with nothing on! he thought. There'll be ladies there! And besides, with my trousers the thieves have taken the rosin which was in them!

He thought for a long time, painfully, till his head ached. Oh! he remembered at last. Not far from the bank, in the bushes, there's a little bridge. . . . I can sit under the bridge until it gets dark, and when night falls I'll creep to the nearest cottage. . . .

Dwelling on this thought, Smychkov put on his top hat, hoisted the double-bass on his back, and trudged along to the bushes. Naked, with the musical instrument on his back, he was reminiscent of some ancient, mythical demi-god.

Now, reader, while my hero is sitting under the bridge and giving himself up to sorrow, let us leave him for a time and turn our attention to the girl who was fishing. What happened to her? When the beauty woke up and did not see the float on the water, she hastened to give her rod a jerk. The rod strained, but the hook and float did not appear from under the water. Evidently Smychkov's bouquet had become sodden in the water, had swollen and grown heavy.

Either there's a big fish caught on it, thought the girl, or else the hook has got entangled.

After jerking the rod a bit more, the girl decided that the hook had got entangled.

What a pity! she thought. And they bite so well in the evening. What shall I do?

And without further ado the eccentric girl threw off her diaphanous clothes and plunged her lovely body in the current right up to her marble shoulders. It was not easy to unhook the bouquet, which had become entangled with the line, but patience and labour won the day. After about a quarter of an hour the beauty came out of the water, radiant and happy, holding the hook in her hand.

But she was in the hands of cruel fortune. The scoundrels who had taken Smychkov's clothes had abducted her dress too, leaving her nothing but a jar full of worms.

What shall I do now? she wept. Must I really go about like this? No, never! Death would be better! I'll wait until it gets dark; then, in the darkness I'll get as far as Agafia's and send her home for a dress. . . . And while I'm waiting I'll hide under the bridge.

Choosing a way where the grass was longest and bending down, my heroine ran to the bridge. When she crawled under the bridge she saw there a naked man with a musical mane and a hairy chest; she gave a cry and fainted.

Smychkov was frightened too. At first he took the girl for a naiad.

Is this a river siren, come to lure me? he thought, and he found this conjecture tempting, for he had always had a very high opinion of his personal appearance. And if she's not a siren, but a human being, how can this strange transformation be explained? Why is she here, under the bridge? And what is the matter with her?

While he was deciding these questions, the beauty came to.

'Don't kill me!' she whispered. 'I am Princess Bibulova. I beseech you! You'll be given a lot of money! I was in the water just now disentangling my hook, and some thieves stole my new dress, shoes and everything!'

'Madam,' said Smychkov in an imploring voice, 'they stole my clothes too. And what's more, together with my trousers they carried off my rosin which was in them!'

Usually no double-bass and trombone players have any presence of mind; Smychkov, however, was a pleasant exception.

'Madam,' he said, after a moment. 'I see that you are embarrassed by my appearance. But, you will agree, I cannot leave this place for the same reasons as yourself. I've got an idea: would you care to lie down in my double-bass case and cover yourself with the lid? That would hide me from you. . . .'

Having said this, Smychkov pulled the double-bass out of its case. For a moment it seemed to him that, in handing over the case, he was profaning Sacred Art, but he did not hesitate for long. The beauty lay down in the case and curled herself up in a ball, while he tightened the straps and began to rejoice that Nature had endowed him with such brains.

'Now, madam, you can't see me,' he said. 'Lie there, and don't worry. When it's dark I'll carry you to your parents' house. I can come back here for the double-bass later.'

When darkness fell Smychkov hoisted the case with the beauty inside it on to his shoulders, and trudged off in the direction of the Bibulovs' villa. His plan was as follows: to begin with, he would go as far as the first cottage and acquire some clothes, and then go on. . . .

Every cloud has a silver lining . . ., he thought, scattering the dust with his bare feet and bending under his burden. Bibulov will probably reward me handsomely for the warm interest I have taken in the princess's fate.

'Are you comfortable, madam?' he asked, in the tone of a *cavalier galant* inviting a lady to a quadrille. 'Please don't stand on ceremony, and do make yourself absolutely at home in my case!'

Suddenly the gallant Smychkov thought he saw two human figures wrapped in darkness walking ahead of him. On looking more closely, he became convinced that this was not an optical illusion: two figures were, in fact, walking along, and were even carrying some sort of bundles in their hands. . . .

I wonder if those are the thieves? the thought flashed through his mind. They're carrying something. It's probably our clothes!

Smychkov put the case down on the road, and started in pursuit of the figures.

'Stop!' he cried. 'Stop! Stop thief!'

The figures looked round and, seeing that they were being pursued, took to their heels. . . . For a long time the princess heard rapid footsteps and cries of 'Stop!' At last all was silent.

Smychkov was carried away by the chase and, probably, the beauty would have had to lie in the field by the road for a good while longer, if it had not been for a happy coincidence. It so happened that at that very time and along that very road Smychkov's friends Zhuchkov, the flautist, and Razmakhaikin, the clarinettist, were walking to the Bibulovs' villa. They stumbled over the case, both looked at each other, and raised their hands in amazement.

'A double-bass!' said Zhuchkov. 'Why, it's our Smychkov's double-bass! But how did it get here?'

'Probably something happened to Smychkov,' decided Razmakhaikin. 'Either he got drunk, or else he was robbed. In any case, it wouldn't be right to leave the double-bass here. Let's take it with us.'

Zhuchkov hoisted the case on his back, and the musicians continued on their way.

'It's the devil of a weight!' the flautist grumbled all the time. 'I would not agree to play a monster like this for anything in the world . . . ugh!'

When they arrived at Prince Bibulov's villa the musicians put the case down in the place reserved for the orchestra, and went to the bar.

The chandeliers and sconces were already lit in the villa. The fiancé, Lakeich, a handsome and attractive official of the Ministry of Transport, was standing in the middle of the ballroom and, with his hands in his pockets, was chatting with Count Shkalikov. They were talking about music.

'You know, Count,' said Lakeich, 'in Naples I was personally acquainted with a violinist who really performed miracles. You wouldn't believe it! On the double-bass . . . on an ordinary double-bass he produced such devilish trills that it was simply amazing! He played Strauss waltzes!'

'Come now, that's impossible,' said the count, sceptically.

'I assure you! He even performed a Liszt rhapsody! I was living in the same hotel as he was, and as I had nothing better to do he taught me how to play a Liszt rhapsody on the double-bass.'

'A Liszt rhapsody! Mmm—you're joking. . . .'

'You don't believe me?' laughed Lakeich. 'Then I'll prove it to you now! Let's go to the orchestra!'

The fiancé and the count went off to the orchestra. They went up to the double-bass, and began quickly to undo the straps . . . and—oh, horror!

But there, while the reader, giving his imagination free rein, pictures the outcome of the musical argument, let us turn to Smychkov. . . . The unfortunate musician did not catch up with the thieves, and when he returned to the place where he had left the case he did not find his valuable burden. Lost in conjecture, he walked up and down the road several times and, not seeing the case, decided that he must be on the wrong road. . . .

This is awful! he thought, tearing his hair, and his blood running cold. She'll suffocate in the case! I'm a murderer!

He walked the roads and searched for the case till midnight, but finally, dead-beat, he went back under the bridge.

I'll have another look at dawn, he decided.

His search at dawn yielded the same result, and Smychkov decided to wait for night under the bridge. . . .

'I'll find her!' he muttered, taking off his top hat and tearing his hair. 'I'll find her, if I have to search for a year!'

And still, so the peasants living in those parts say, at night near the bridge a nude man may be seen, overgrown with hair and wearing a top hat. Now and again, from under the bridge, can be heard the rumble of a double-bass.

A VISIT TO FRIENDS

A LETTER came one morning:

Dear Misha, You have quite forgotten us, do come as soon as you can, we want to see you. We both implore you on bended knee, come to-day, show us the light of your countenance. Awaiting you with impatience.

Ta and Va.

Kuzminki, 7th June.

The letter was from Tatyana Alexeyevna Losev who, some ten or twelve years ago when Podgorin had been living in Kuzminki, had been known as Ta for short. But who was Va? Podgorin recalled long talks, gay laughter, youthful crushes, walks in the evening, and a whole flower-bed of young girls who used to live in and near Kuzminki, and he recalled a simple, lively, intelligent face with freckles that went so well with the dark copper of the hair—that was Varya or Varvara Pavlovna, Tatyana's friend. She had taken a degree in medicine and was working in a factory somewhere near Tula, and now, apparently, had gone to Kuzminki on a visit.

Dear Va! thought Podgorin, giving himself up to memories. How nice she is!

Tatyana, Varya and he were almost of the same age; but at that time he had been a student, while they were grown-up, marriageable young girls, and regarded him as a boy. And though by now he was a lawyer and his hair was going grey, they still called him Misha and considered him young, and said that he had not yet experienced anything in life.

He loved them dearly, but probably loved them more in retrospect than in actual fact. He knew little of their present

life, had no understanding for it, and felt it to be alien to him.
Alien, too, was this short, skittish letter, which had probably
cost them a great deal of time and strain to compose, and
while Tatyana was writing, her husband, Sergei Sergeich,
was probably standing behind her. . . . She had received
Kuzminki as her dowry only six years before, but it was
already ruined by this same Sergei Sergeich, and now, every
time they had to pay the bank or pay interest on the mortgage,
they turned to Podgorin for advice because he was a lawyer;
indeed, they had twice already asked him for a loan. Now,
too, they obviously wanted either his advice or his money.

He no longer had any desire to go to Kuzminki as he used
to in the old days. It was sad there. Gone were the laughter
and the noise and the gay, carefree faces, and trysts on calm
moonlit nights, and gone, above all, was youth; and anyway,
it was all probably charming in retrospect only. . . . Apart
from Ta and Va there was also Na, Tatyana's sister Nadejda,
whom in fun and in earnest they used to call his betrothed;
he had seen her grow up, they had counted on him marrying
her, and at one time he had been in love with her and was
going to propose to her—but she was twenty-four by now,
and he was still unmarried. . . .

Strange, the way it all turned out, he mused now, re-
reading the letter in some perplexity. But I couldn't not go,
they'd be hurt. . . .

The fact that he had not visited the Losevs for a long time
weighed on his conscience. And after walking up and down
his room and giving some thought to it, he made an effort
and decided to go and spend about three days with them,
perform that service and then be free and have a clean
conscience, at least till summer. And, making ready after
lunch to go to Brest station, he told the servant that he would
be back in three days' time.

It was a two hours' railway journey from Moscow to
Kuzminki, and then a ride of some twenty minutes in a
horse-carriage from the station. There was a view, from the

station, of Tatyana's wood and of the three narrow villas
begun—but never finished—by Losev who, during the first
few years of marriage had ventured into all sorts of specula-
tive deals. His ruin was caused by these villas and by all
kinds of business enterprises, and by frequent visits to Moscow, where he lunched at the Slavyanski Bazaar, dined at
the Hermitage and finished his day in the Malaya Bronnaya
Street or the Zhivoderka with the gipsy singers (he called
this 'shaking himself up'). Podgorin, too, used to drink,
sometimes a great deal, and used to visit women without
being too particular about it, but he did it lazily and coldly,
experiencing no pleasure; and he had a feeling of repulsion
when others in his presence gave themselves up to it with
passion, he did not understand people who felt themselves
freer in Zhivorderka than they did at home with decent
women, and he did not like such people; he had the
impression that every kind of uncleanliness stuck to them like
a thistle. And he did not like Losev, and considered him
uninteresting, no good at anything, lazy, and often had a
feeling of repulsion in his company. . . .

Just after he had passed the wood he was met by Sergei
Sergeich and Nadejda.

'My dear fellow, why have you forgotten us?' said Sergei
Sergeich, kissing him three times and then holding him by
the waist with both hands. 'You don't love us any more, old
friend!'

He had large features, a fat nose and a sparse beard; he
brushed his hair sideways, merchant-fashion, in order to
appear simple and purely Russian. When he talked he
breathed straight in the face of the person he was speaking
to, and when silent breathed heavily through his nose. His
body, well-fed and replete to superfluity, constrained his
movements, and in order to ease his breathing he constantly
puffed out his chest, and this gave him a haughty air. By his
side his sister-in-law, Nadejda, appeared ethereal. She was
a light blonde, pale, slender, with kind, affectionate eyes;

Podgorin could not make out whether she was pretty or not, for he had known her from childhood and was used to her appearance. Now she was wearing a white dress with an open neck, and this impression of a long, bare, white neck was new to him and not quite pleasant.

'My sister and the rest of us have been expecting you ever since this morning,' she said. 'Varya is staying with us and is also expecting you'.

She took his arm and suddenly laughed for no reason and let out a light, joyful cry, as if suddenly charmed by some thought. The field, with its flowering rye motionless in the still air, and the wood lit up by the sun, were beautiful; and it looked as if Nadejda had noticed it only now, as she was walking by Podgorin's side.

'I have come to spend three days with you,' he said. 'You must forgive me, I couldn't get away from Moscow any earlier.'

'Bad, bad, you have forgotten us,' Sergei Sergeich reproached him good-naturedly. 'Jamais de ma vie!' he said suddenly, and snapped his fingers.

He had a habit, when the person he was speaking to was not expecting it, of saying a phrase by way of exclamation which bore no relation to the conversation, and of snapping his fingers as he said it. And he was always imitating somebody; if he rolled his eyes, or carelessly tossed his hair back, or spoke with pathos, it meant that the day before he had been to the theatre or to a dinner at which speeches were made. Now he was walking as if suffering from gout, taking small steps and not bending his knees—probably imitating someone again.

'You know, Tanya did not believe you'd come,' said Nadejda. 'But Varya and I had a premonition; I knew somehow that you'd arrive by just this train.'

'Jamais de ma vie!' repeated Sergei Sergeich.

The ladies were waiting for them on the terrace in the garden. Ten years ago Podgorin—he was a poor university student then—used to teach Nadejda mathematics and history in exchange for board and lodging; and Varya, then a girl student, had profited by this opportunity to take Latin lessons from him. But Tanya, already then a beautiful grown-up girl, thought of nothing but love, and wanted only love and happiness, wanted them passionately, and waited for a husband and dreamt about him day and night. And now, when she was already over thirty, just as beautiful and striking as ever, dressed in a wide gown, her arms full and white, she thought only of her husband and of her two little girls, and her expression seemed to signify that though she now was talking and smiling, she was keeping her thoughts to herself all the same, that she was mounting guard over her love and her rights to that love, and was ready at any moment to attack any foe who might wish to deprive her of her husband and children. Her love was strong and, she thought, mutual, but jealousy and fear for the children were constantly tormenting her and prevented her from being happy.

After the noisy greetings on the terrace everyone, except Sergei Sergeich, went to Tatyana's room. The rays of the sun did not penetrate there through the drawn blinds, and the room was plunged into semi-darkness, so that all the roses gathered in a large bunch appeared to have the same colour. Podgorin was made to sit in an old armchair next to the window. Nadejda sat down at his feet on a low stool. He knew that besides the affectionate reproaches, fun and laughter which were heard now and which reminded him so much of the past, there would also be an unpleasant conversation about bills and mortgages—that was unavoidable—and he thought that it might, perhaps, be better to have the business talk at once, without putting it off till later; get it over quickly, and then—out into the garden and the fresh air. . . .

'Shall we talk business first?' he said. 'Anything new in Kuzminki? Is something rotten in the state of Denmark?'

'We are in trouble here in Kuzminki,' replied Tatyana, and sighed sadly. 'Oh, we are in such difficulties, in such difficulties that I don't think we could be in greater difficulties,' she said, and paced up and down the room in her excitement. 'Our estate is being sold, the auction is fixed for 7th August, it's been advertised everywhere, and buyers come here, walk about the rooms, look round. . . . Everyone now has the right to enter my room and have a look round. Legally this is just, perhaps, but I feel deeply humiliated and offended. We have no money and we can no longer borrow. In short, it's terrible, terrible! I swear to you,' she continued, her voice trembling and tears gushing out of her eyes, 'I swear to you by everything that's sacred, by my children's happiness, I cannot live without Kuzminki! I was born here, this is my nest and if it's taken away from me I shall not survive it, I'll die from sheer despair.'

'I think you take too gloomy a view,' said Podgorin. 'Everything will turn out all right. Your husband will find a job, you will start afresh, you'll begin a new life.'

'How can you say that?' cried Tatyana; now she looked very beautiful and strong, and the fact that she was ready at any moment to pounce on the foe who would want to deprive her of husband, children and nest was expressed particularly bluntly on her face and her whole body. 'New life, indeed! Sergei is trying to get a job, he has been promised the job of an Inland Revenue inspector somewhere in the Ufa or Perm Province, and I am ready to go anywhere—to Siberia, if necessary—I'm ready to live there ten, twenty years, but I must know that sooner or later I shall finish up by returning to Kuzminki. I can't live without Kuzminki. I can't, and I won't. I won't!' she cried and stamped her foot.

'You are a lawyer, Misha,' said Varya, 'you're a bit of a wangler and it is your job to give advice as to what to do next.'

There was only one fair and reasonable answer: nothing can be done, but Podgorin did not have the heart to say so frankly, and mumbled haltingly:

'It'll have to be considered. . . . I will think.'

There were two men inside him. As a lawyer he had occasionally to deal with coarse subjects, in court rooms and with clients his behaviour was haughty, and he was always forthright and trenchant when expressing an opinion, and when he went on the razzle with other men he did it crudely. But with close friends and people he had known for a long time he was extraordinarily considerate, was shy and sensitive, and did not know how to be forthright. One tear, an unfriendly glance, a lie or even an ugly gesture was enough to make him shrink and lose his will-power. Now Nadejda was sitting at his feet, and he did not like her bare neck; this embarrassed him, and he even wanted to go home. Once, a year ago, he had met Sergei Sergeich in a lady's flat in Bronnaya Street, and he now felt ill at ease with Tatyana, as if he had himself been party to this infidelity. And this conversation about Kuzminki put him in a very awkward situation. He was used to the fact that all ticklish and unpleasant problems were solved by judges or the jury, or simply by some legal clause; but whenever a problem was put up to him for his own personal solution he became confused.

'Misha, you are a friend, we all love you as one of the family,' Tatyana continued, 'and I tell you frankly: we are putting all our hopes on you. For God's sake tell us what to do. Should we send in an application somewhere, perhaps? Perhaps it isn't too late to transfer the estate legally to Nadya or Varya? . . . What should we do?'

'Come to the rescue, Misha, do,' said Varya, lighting a cigarette. 'You have always been intelligent. You haven't lived much, haven't had any experience of life, but you have a good head on your shoulders . . . you'll help Tanya, I know. . . .'

'I'll have to think . . . perhaps I'll think of something.'

They went for a walk in the garden and in the fields. Sergei Sergeich went out for a walk with them too. He took

Podgorin's arm and was all the time dragging him on to walk in front, apparently wanting to talk to him about something, probably about the unsatisfactory money matters. But to walk next to Sergei Sergeich and talk to him was sheer torment. He constantly kissed you, and did it three times on each occasion, took you by the arm, put his arm round your waist, breathed in your face, and gave the impression of being covered with a sweet glue and just about to stick to you; and the expression in his eyes which meant that he needed something from Podgorin, and that he was at any moment going to ask for something, was most distressing— just as if he were aiming a revolver at you.

The sun set, it was getting dark. Here and there along the railway line lights were lit, green, red. . . . Varya stopped, and looking at the lights, began reciting:

> ' "Straight lies the railway, with narrow slopes
>   banking it,
>   Bridges, and fence-posts, and rails,
>   And, all along, there are Russian bones flanking
>   it . . .
>   Many, how many! . . ." '

'How does it go on? Good heavens! I've forgotten it all!'

> ' "There were we straining in winter-time, summer-
>   time,
>   Bent were our backs, ever bent . . ." '

She recited with feeling in a beautiful, rich voice; her cheeks glowed and tears stood in her eyes. This was the old Varya, Varya the student, and listening to her Podgorin thought of the past and remembered that when he was a student he too used to know a lot of good poetry by heart and had liked reciting it.

> ' "No more unbending his back hunched so crookedly,
>   Now he keeps silence, is dumb evermore . . ." '

3

But Varya could remember no further. . . . She was
silent, and smiled wanly a weak smile, and now she had
finished reciting the green and red lights looked sad. . . .

'Oh, I've forgotten!'

But then Podgorin suddenly remembered—it had somehow stuck in his memory from his student days—and recited
quietly, in a half-whisper:

' "People of Russia have lived through enough,
   Lived through this railway, too, while they were
      making it,
   Will live through all—and at long last, victorious,
   Hew out a road, broad and clear, coming through . . .
   Only it's sad . . ." '

'Only it's sad,' Varya interrupted him as she remembered,
'Only it's sad that this epoch so glorious, will not be lived in
by me, or by you!'

And she laughed and clapped him on the shoulder.

They went home and sat down to supper. Sergei Sergeich
negligently tucked a corner of his napkin behind his collar,
in imitation of someone.

'Let's have a drink,' he said, pouring out a vodka for
himself and Podgorin. 'We old students, we could drink and
act and wax eloquent. I drink to your health, old friend, and
you, you must drink to the health of an old fool of an idealist,
and wish him to remain an idealist till his death. In cases
like mine, the grave is the only physician.'

Throughout dinner Tatyana threw tender glances at her
husband, felt jealous and worried that he might eat or drink
something that was bad for him. She was under the impression that he was spoilt by women, and tired—she found this
attractive in him, but at the same time she suffered. Varya
and Nadya also dealt with him tenderly and looked at him
with a worried expression, as if afraid that he would suddenly
leave them. When he wanted to pour himself out another
glass Varya frowned and said:

'You are poisoning yourself, Sergei Sergeich. You are a nervous, impressionable man and can easily become a dipsomaniac. Tanya, have the vodka taken away.'

In general, Sergei Sergeich had a great success with women. They liked his tall figure, his well-built frame, his large features, his idleness and his misfortunes. They said he was very kind and therefore a spendthrift; that he was an idealist and therefore impractical; that he was honest, pure-hearted, unable to adapt himself to men and circumstances, and that therefore he had nothing and had never found a steady job. They had a deep faith in him, adored him and spoilt him with their worship, so that he now himself believed that he was an idealist, impractical, honest, pure-hearted, and that he was head and shoulders above, and better than, these women.

'Don't you think they are lovely, my little girls?' Tatyana said, looking lovingly at her two girls—healthy, well-fed, for all the world like a couple of buns—and giving them platefuls of rice. 'You have a good look at them! They say all mothers praise their children, but I assure you I am being objective, my girls are quite extraordinary; especially the elder.'

Podgorin was smiling at her and at the girls, but he found it strange that that healthy, young and intelligent woman, a big complex organism really, should be spending all her energies, all her vitality on such a simple and trivial task as the building-up of a nest which anyway had already been built up.

Perhaps this is how it should be, he thought, but it is neither interesting nor intelligent.

'He had the bear on top of him before he could say "Knife",' said Sergei Sergeich, and snapped his fingers.

They finished supper. Tatyana and Varya made Podgorin sit on the sofa in the drawing-room and spoke to him in a low voice, again about business matters.

'We must come to Sergei Sergeich's rescue,' said Varya, 'it's our moral duty. He has his weaknesses, he is not thrifty,

doesn't think of the rainy day, but that's because he is kind
and generous. He has the heart of a child. If you give him a
million he will have nothing left in a month; he'll have given
it all away.'

'That's right, that's right,' said Tatyana, and tears flowed
down her cheeks. 'He has made me suffer a lot, but I must
say he is a wonderful man.'

And both of them, Tatyana and Varya, could not restrain
themselves from reproaching Podgorin a little cruelly:

'But your generation, Misha, is no longer the same!

What has my generation got to do with it? thought
Podgorin. After all, Losev is about six years older than I am,
no more. . . .

'Life is no easy matter,' said Varya and sighed. 'Man is
always threatened with some loss or other. Either they want
to take your estate away from you, or else a member of your
family falls ill and you are afraid he might die—and so it is,
day in, day out. And there's nothing we can do about it, my
friends. We must submit uncomplainingly to the Supreme
Will, we must remember that nothing in this world is
fortuitous; everything has its distant aims. You, Misha, you
haven't lived much yet and haven't suffered much, and
you'll laugh at me; do, by all means, but I'll still say: at the
time of my bitterest worries, I experienced several cases of
clairvoyance, and this has stirred me to the innermost
depths of my being, and now I know that nothing is fortuitous,
and that all that happens in our life is essential.

How unlike Varya the student, the red-haired, gay, noisy,
daring Varya was this Varya, grey-haired by now, tightly
laced into her corset, dressed in a fashionable dress with high
sleeves, Varya, rolling a cigarette in her long, bony fingers
which trembled for some reason, Varya, so readily lapsing
into mysticism and speaking in such a lifeless and monotonous way. . . .

And where is it all gone now! thought Podgorin, feeling
bored as he listened to her.

'Sing something, Va,' he said to her, so as to stop this conversation about clairvoyance. 'You used to sing well in the old days.'

'Oh, Misha, that's all gone and finished now.'

'Well then, recite something from Nekrasov.'

'I've forgotten everything. I did it quite spontaneously just now.'

In spite of the corset and the high sleeves, it was obvious that she was living in want and was leading a starveling existence in her factory near Tula. And it was very obvious that she had overworked herself; hard, monotonous toil, constant interference in other people's affairs and care for others had tired her out and aged her, and Podgorin, looking now at her sad, already faded face, thought that it was not Kuzminki or Sergei Sergeich, on whose behalf she took so much trouble, that should really be helped, but she herself.

University education and the fact that she had become a doctor, seemed not to have touched the woman in her. She liked weddings, confinements, christenings, long conversations about children, quite as much as Tatyana did; she liked thrillers with a happy ending, and in newspapers read only about fires, floods, and grand ceremonies; she very much wanted Podgorin to propose to Nadejda, and had that happened she would have cried from sheer emotion.

He did not know whether it happened by chance or whether Varya had prearranged it—he remained alone with Nadejda; but the mere suspicion that he was being watched and that something was expected of him embarrassed and disconcerted him, and in Nadejda's company he felt as if they had been put together in the same cage.

'Let's go out into the garden,' she said.

They went out into the garden: he—moody and annoyed, not knowing what to talk to her about, and she—beaming with joy, proud that he was near her, obviously pleased that he was staying for another three days and full, perhaps, of sweet dreams and hopes. He did not know whether she loved him, but he knew that she had long ago grown used and attached to him, and still regarded him as her tutor, and that the emotions that now filled her heart were the same as her sister Tatyana's had once been, that, in other words, she thought of nothing but love, of how to get married as quickly as possible, have a husband, children and her own home.

'It's getting dark,' he said.

'Yes. The moon rises very late.'

They kept on walking along the same drive, near the house. Podgorin did not want to go deeper into the garden: it was dark there, he would have to take Nadejda's arm, be very near to her. Some shadows were moving on the terrace, and he had the feeling it was Tatyana and Varya watching him.

'I must ask your advice,' said Nadejda, standing still. 'If Kuzminki is sold, Sergei Sergeich will work in an office, and then our life must change completely. I'll not go with my sister, we shall part because I don't want to be a burden to her family. I must work. I'll find some job in Moscow, will earn something and will help my sister and her husband. You'll help me with your advice, won't you?'

Quite ignorant of toil, she was now inspired by the thought of an independent, toiling life, and was building plans for the future—so much was written on her face; and a life during which she would be working and helping others seemed to her beautiful and romantic. He saw near him her pale face and black eyebrows, and remembered what an intelligent and clever pupil she had been, what great gifts she had and how pleasant it had been to give her lessons. And probably even now she was not just a young lady looking for a husband, but an intelligent, noble-minded girl, uncommonly kind, with a meek and gentle soul which could be moulded like wax into any shape, and in a suitable environment she would make an excellent woman.

Why shouldn't I marry her, really? thought Podgorin, but for some reason the thought frightened him and he went back to the house.

Tatyana was sitting at the piano in the drawing-room, and her playing reminded him vividly of the past, when in that very drawing-room people had played, sung and danced till late at night, with the windows open, and the birds in the garden and near the river had sung too. Podgorin cheered up, began romping about, danced with both Nadejda and Varya, and then sang. A corn on his foot worried him and he asked for permission to put on Sergei Sergeich's slippers, and oddly enough, in those slippers he felt himself to be a member of the household, a relative (Just like a brother-in-law—the thought flashed through his mind), and he cheered up even more. At the sight of him they all revived, brightened up and became almost younger. Their faces all shone with hope: Kuzminki was saved! It was so easy, after all: all that had to be done was to think of something, to search through the laws a bit, or for Nadya to marry Podgorin. . . . And obviously things were already beginning to point that way. Nadya, pink and happy, her eyes full of tears, in expectation of something unusual, was whirling round as she danced and her white dress billowed about her and revealed her small, pretty feet in flesh-coloured stockings. . . . Varya, very pleased, took Podgorin's arm and wearing a significant expression said to him in a half-whisper:

'Misha, don't run away from your own happiness. Take it while it offers itself of its own accord; later on you will be running after it, but it'll be too late, you won't catch it.'

Podgorin wanted to make promises and encourage hopes, and he was himself ready to believe that Kuzminki was saved and that it was so simple to do.

' "And of this earth you'll be the queen",' he began to sing, striking an attitude, but he suddenly remembered that he could do nothing for those people, nothing at all, and fell silent, feeling guilty.

And afterwards he sat silently in a corner with his feet in borrowed slippers tucked up under him.

At the sight of him the others, too, understood that nothing more could be done, and became silent and quiet. Someone closed the piano. And they all noticed that it was late, time to go to bed, and Tatyana put out the big lamp in the drawing-room.

Podgorin's bed had been made ready for him in the annexe he had formerly lived in. Sergei Sergeich took him there, holding a candle high above his head, although the moon was already rising and it was light. They were going along a drive with lilac bushes on either side, and the gravel was scrunching under their feet.

'He had the bear on top of him before he could say "knife",' said Sergei Sergeich.

And Podgorin had the impression of having heard this phrase a thousand times before. How tired he was of it! When they had reached the annexe Sergei Sergeich got a bottle and two glasses out of his ample jacket and stood them on the table.

'That's brandy,' he said. 'Number o o. In the house there's Varya; you can't drink when she's there, she launches forth about dipsomania right away, but here we can do what we please. The brandy is superb.'

They sat down. The brandy turned out to be really good.

'Let's drink thoroughly to-night,' continued Sergei Sergeich, sucking a lemon. 'I was a student in my day, and like to shake myself up sometimes. It's essential.'

But in his eyes there was the same expression as before, that he needed something from Podgorin and that he was about to ask for something.

'Let's drink, my friend,' he continued with a sigh. 'Life has become intolerable without it. It's all over for cranks like me—finished. Idealism is not the fashion nowadays. The rouble is king now, and if you don't want to be shoved out of the way, fall down on your face and worship the rouble. But I can't. It just makes me sick.'

'When's the date of the auction?' asked Podgorin to change the subject.

'The seventh of August. But I haven't the slightest intention of saving Kuzminki, my dear fellow. We are very badly in arrears on the mortgage and the estate brings in no income at all, nothing but a loss every year. It isn't worth it. . . . Tanya is sorry of course, it's her ancestral home, but I am even pleased to a certain extent, to tell you the truth. I'm not a country dweller. A big, noisy city is my field, struggle is my element!'

He said other things too, but never what he wanted to say, and watched Podgorin closely as if waiting for a suitable moment. And suddenly Podgorin saw his eyes close to him, felt his breath on his face. . . .

'My dear fellow, save me!' said Sergei Sergeich, breathing heavily. 'Give me two hundred roubles! I implore you!'

Podgorin wanted to say that he was himself hard up, and thought that it would be better to give these two hundred roubles to a pauper or even merely to lose them at cards, but he felt terribly shy; he felt himself trapped in that little room with its one candle, wanted to get rid as quickly as possible of that breath, of those soft hands which were holding his waist and seemed to have already stuck to him, and he quickly began to search his pockets for the diary in which he kept his money.

'There you are . . .' he mumbled, taking out a hundred roubles. 'I'll let you have the rest afterwards. I have no more with me. You see, I don't know how to refuse,' he went on irritably, his anger mounting. 'I have an execrable feminine nature. Only please let me have this money back. I am short of cash too.'

'Thank you, thank you, friend!'

'And for God's sake stop imagining that you are an

idealist. You are as much of an idealist as I am a turkey cock. You are just a thoughtless idler and no more.'

Sergei Sergeich heaved a deep sigh and sat down on the sofa.

'You are annoyed, my dear fellow,' he said, 'but if you knew how hard it is for me! I am living through a dreadful time now. My dear fellow, I swear it's not myself I'm sorry for, oh no! I'm sorry for my wife and children. If it wasn't for the children and my wife I'd have done away with myself long ago.'

And suddenly his head and shoulders shook and he began to sob.

'That's the last straw!' said Podgorin, walking about the room in his agitation and feeling very annoyed. 'What can be done with a man who has done a lot of evil and then sobs? These tears of yours disarm one, I haven't got it in me to say anything to you. You sob, therefore you are right.'

'I have done a lot of evil?' asked Sergei Sergeich, getting up and looking at Podgorin in surprise. 'My dear fellow, is that you saying it? I have done a lot of evil? Oh, how little you know me! How little you understand me!'

'All right, let's assume I don't understand you, only please don't sob. It's disgusting.'

'Oh, how little you know me!' Losev was repeating, in all sincerity. 'How little you know me!'

'Look at yourself in the glass,' continued Podgorin. 'You are not a young man any more, you'll be old soon, it's about time you gave some thought to your behaviour, time you realised a little who you are and what you are. Doing nothing all your life, all your life this idle, childish prattle, poses and affectation—I'm surprised your head's not spinning and you aren't tired of living so. You're a depressing man to be with! One gets into a mental torpor in your company out of sheer boredom!'

Having said this, Podgorin left the annexe and slammed the door. Probably for the first time in his life he had been sincere and had said what he wanted.

But only a little later he was sorry for having been so stern. What was the use of speaking seriously or arguing with a man who constantly lied, ate a lot, drank a lot, spent a lot of other people's money, and at the same time was convinced that he was an idealist and a martyr? This case was one of stupidity or bad habits which had gone on for a long time, had bitten deep into the man's organism like a disease and was by now incurable. Anyway, indignation and stern reproaches were of no use here—laughter would be more in place; one good jibe would do a great deal more than a dozen sermons!

Even simpler would be to pay no attention at all, thought Podgorin, and above all not to give money.

And then in a little while he no longer thought either about Sergei Sergeich or his hundred roubles. The night was quiet and still and very light. Whenever on moonlit nights Podgorin looked at the sky it always seemed to him that nothing was awake except the moon and himself, and that all else was either asleep or dozing; and his thoughts refused to busy themselves with either men or money, and his mood gradually became quiet and peaceful; he felt alone in the world, and in the stillness of the night the sound of his own footsteps seemed to him so sad.

The garden was surrounded by a white stone wall. In the right-hand corner of the side facing a field stood a tower built a long time ago at the time of the serfs. The lower part was made of stone and the upper part of timber, with a platform, a conical roof and a tall spire on which could be seen the black shape of the weather-vane. There were two doors at the bottom, which made it possible to go straight from the garden into the field, and a staircase which creaked under one's footsteps, leading up to the platform. Broken old armchairs were thrown together in a heap under the staircase, and the moonlight which now penetrated through the doorway lit up these armchairs, and they, with their little curved legs sticking up in the air, seemed to have come to life and to be lying in wait for someone in the stillness of the night.

Podgorin went up the stairs to the platform and sat down. Immediately on the other side of the wall there was a dividing ditch with a bank, and beyond was the field, wide and floodlit by the rays of the moon. Podgorin knew that there was a wood directly in front of him, about two miles away from the park, and now he imagined he saw a dark streak in the distance. Corncrakes and quails were crying; and coming from the direction of the wood he could hear a cuckoo which, too, was awake.

He heard footsteps. Somebody was walking in the garden and was approaching the tower.

A dog began to bark.

'Beetle!' a woman's voice called quietly. 'Beetle, come back!'

He heard someone entering the tower, and a minute later a black dog—an old friend of Podgorin's—appeared on the bank of the ditch. It stopped, looked up in the direction where Podgorin was sitting, and began wagging its tail in friendly gesture. And then a little later, a white figure rose up from the ditch like a shadow and also stopped on the bank. It was Nadejda.

'What do you see there?' she asked the dog and peered up.

She did not see Podgorin, but probably felt his near presence, for she was smiling and her pale face lit up by the moon seemed happy. The tower's black shadow stretching along the earth far into the field, the motionless white figure with a blissful smile on a pale face, the black dog, the shadows of both, and the whole thing together something like a dream.

'There's no one there,' said Nadejda quietly.

She stood and waited for him to come down and call her and tell her all that was on his mind, for them both to be happy in this still and beautiful night. White, pale, slender, very beautiful in the moonlight, she was waiting for affection;

her constant dreams of happiness and love had worn her out, and she was no longer capable of concealing her feelings, and the whole of her figure and the brightness of her eyes and the happy smile congealed on her lips, betrayed her innermost thoughts; but he felt embarrassed, shrank within himself, and sat quietly, not knowing whether he should speak up in order to treat it all as a joke afterwards, or whether he should keep silent, and he was annoyed and thought only of the fact that there in the park, on a moonlit night, by the side of a beautiful, lovelorn, dreamy girl, he was just as indifferent as he was in the Malaya Bronnaya Street—obviously because both the poetry and the coarse prose of life were equally dead for him. Dead, too, were trysts and moonlit nights, and white figures with slender waists, and mysterious shadows, and towers and parks, and such 'types' as Sergei Sergeich and such as himself, Podgorin, with his cold boredom, constant annoyance, inability to adapt himself to real life, inability to take from it what it was capable of giving, the exhausting, aching thirst for what did not and could not exist on earth. And now, sitting there in that tower, he would have preferred a good firework display, or some procession in the moonlight, or Varya who would have recited 'The Railway', or another woman who, standing on the bank where Nadejda was now standing, would be telling him something interesting and new, bearing no relation to either love or happiness, and even if she had been talking of love it would be a call to new forms of life, lofty and rational, on the eve of which we are now living, and of whose existence we sometimes have a premonition. . . .

'There's no one there,' said Nadejda.

And after standing and waiting for another minute, she went quietly, with bowed head, in the direction of the wood. The dog ran on in front. And for a long time Podgorin could see a white spot.

'Strange, the way it has all turned out, really . . .' he repeated to himself on his way back to the annexe.

He could not imagine what he would talk about with Sergei Sergeich and Tatyana and how he would behave towards Nadejda the following day, or the day after either—and in anticipation of it he felt embarrassment, fear and boredom. How could he fill in the three long days he had promised to stay there? He recalled the conversation about clairvoyance and Sergei Sergeich's phrase: 'He had the bear on top of him before he could say "knife",' he remembered that to-morrow, in order to please Tatyana, he would have to smile to her replete, podgy little girls—and he decided to leave.

At half-past five Sergei Sergeich, in a bukhara dressing-gown and a tasselled fez, appeared on the terrace of the big house. Without wasting a minute, Podgorin came up to him and began saying good-bye.

'I must be in Moscow by ten o'clock,' he said, without looking at him. 'I quite forgot that I was expected at the solicitor's. Please let me go. As soon as your people are up, make my excuses to them. I am terribly sorry. . . .'

He did not hear what Sergei Sergeich was saying to him and did not look back at the windows of the big house for fear that the ladies might wake up and detain him. He was ashamed of being so nervous. He felt that that was the last time he would ever be in Kuzminki, and that he would never go there again, and as he was driving off he looked back several times at the annexe, where in the past he had spent so many happy days—but within him he felt cold and felt no sadness.

On his table at home the first thing he saw was the note which he had received the previous day. 'Dear Misha,' he read. 'You have quite forgotten us, do come as soon as you can. . . .' And for some reason he remembered how Nadejda had whirled round as she danced, how her dress had billowed about her and revealed her feet in flesh-coloured stockings. . . .

But in another ten minutes he was sitting at his table, working, and no longer thought about Kuzminki.

APPROPRIATE MEASURES

❋

THE small provincial town, which, as the local prison superintendent had once put it, could not be distinguished on any map even under a telescope, is lit up by the mid-day sun. Peace and quiet everywhere. A sanitary commission consisting of the town doctor, the police inspector, two representatives of the Town Council and one trade deputy is slowly proceeding from the Town Hall towards the shopping quarter. Constables follow respectfully behind. . . . The way of the Commission, like the way to Hell, is paved with good intentions. As they walk along, gesticulating, the sanitary inspectors discuss uncleanliness, stink, appropriate measures and other unsavoury subjects. The discussions are so clever that the police inspector walking in front of the group is suddenly seized with delight, turns round and declares:

'We really should try to meet as often as we can and discuss matters! It's a pleasure and an entertainment. As it is, all we do is quarrel. We do, really.'

'Whom shall we begin with, Anikita Nikolaich?' asks the trade deputy, addressing himself to the doctor in the tone of an executioner selecting a victim.

'What about starting off with Osheynikov's shop? Firstly, the man's a scoundrel, and . . . secondly, it's time he was got at. I had some buckwheat from him the other day, and I found rat droppings in it, if you'll pardon the expression. . . . My wife couldn't eat it.'

'Well then, we might as well start off with Osheynikov as with anyone else,' says the doctor with complete indifference.

The inspectors walk into a shop labelled 'Tea, Sugar,

Coffee and other Groceries. A. M. Osheynikov,' and immediately, without further ado, begin their inspection.

'Er . . . yes . . .' says the doctor, looking at attractively piled up pyramids of laundry soap. 'Regular Towers of Babel you've built here! Very ingenuous, I must say! Oh, eh, eh! What's all this? Just look at him! Look at Demyan Gavrilych cutting soap and bread with the same knife!'

'That won't give people cholera, Anikita Nikolaich!' says the shopkeeper reasonably.

'That's true enough, but it's disgusting all the same! After all, I buy bread here, too.'

'We have a special knife for the better sort of customer. Don't you worry, sir. . . .'

The police inspector peers short-sightedly at a ham, scratches it for a long time with his nail, smells it loudly, then taps it with his finger and asks:

'You never have these with strichines in, have you?'

'What a thing to say, sir. . . . Come, come now . . . as if I could!'

The police inspector is overcome with embarrassment, leaves the ham and peers at the price list of Asmolov & Co. The trade deputy puts his hand into a barrel containing buckwheat and feels something soft and velvety. . . . He has a look, and tenderness spreads over his face.

'Pussies . . . pussies! My little darlings!' he murmurs. 'Lying in the buckwheat with their little faces up . . . all cuddly. . . . Now, Demyan Gavrilych, you might send me just one little kitten!'

'Of course, sir. . . . Well and here you have the delicatessen counter, in case you want to inspect it. . . . Herrings here . . . cheese . . . cured sturgeon this is. . . . The sturgeon I got on Thursday, the best kind. . . . Mishka, give me a knife!'

The sanitary inspectors cut themselves a piece of cured sturgeon each, smell it and taste it.

'I might as well have a snack too, while we're about

it . . .' says the grocer, Demyan Gavrilych, as if to himself. 'I had a little bottle lying about somewhere. Ought to have a drink before eating the sturgeon. . . . Gives it a different taste then. . . . Let's have the bottle, Mishka.'

Mishka, his cheeks blown out and eyes popping out of his head, uncorks the bottle and puts it on the counter with a resounding bang.

'Drink on an empty stomach . . .' says the police inspector scratching his head, unable to make up his mind. 'However, if we just have one each. . . . Only you be quick, Demyan Gavrilych, you and your vodka; we're busy!'

A quarter of an hour later the sanitary inspectors, wiping their lips and picking their teeth with match sticks make their way to Golorybenko's shop. As if to spite them, the way here is blocked. . . . Half a dozen young stalwarts, their faces red and sweaty, are rolling a keg of butter out of the shop.

'Keep to the right! . . . Pull it by the rim. . . . Go on. Pull, pull! Put a bit of wood underneath. . . . Oh, damn! Get out of the way, sir, we might crush your toes!'

The barrel sticks in the doorway and stops. . . . The young stalwarts strain away at it and push it and pull it with all their might, puffing and snorting noisily and swearing at the top of their voices. After such efforts, in the course of which the air becomes considerably polluted by the puffing and the snorting, the barrel at last rolls out, but for some unknown reason, rolls back again in defiance of all natural laws, and once more sticks in the doorway. The puffing and snorting begins anew.

'Oh, blast!' exclaims the police inspector. 'Let's got to Shibukin. These devils will be puffing away at it all day.'

The sanitary inspectors find Shibukin's shop locked.

'But it was open!' say the sanitary inspectors, looking at each other in astonishment. 'As we were going into Osheini-kov's shop, Shibukin was standing on the threshold and was

washing out a copper teapot. Where is he?' they ask a
beggar standing near the locked shop.

'Spare a copper for a poor cripple, in the name of God,'
wheezes the beggar. 'Many thanks to you, Guv'nors . . .
bless you and your parents.'

The sanitary inspectors wave him away—and continue on
their way, all except the Town Council representative
Plyunin. He gives the beggar a kopek, crosses himself hastily
as if afraid of something and runs off in pursuit of the rest
of the company.

About two hours later the commission is wending its way
back. The sanitary inspectors look tired and worn out. They
have not laboured in vain; a constable strides solemnly along
carrying a large tray full of rotten apples.

'Well now, after our righteous labours, a bit of a sniffter
might not be a bad idea,' says the police inspector, glancing
at a signboard: "Wine and vodka cellar". 'We need something
to give us back our strength. Er—yes, might do us some good.
Let's go in if you like!'

The sanitary inspectors go down into the cellar and sit
down round a table with bent legs. The police inspector nods
to the bar-keeper, and a bottle appears on the table.

'Pity one can't have a snack with it,' says the trade
deputy, making a wry face as he empties a glass. 'Haven't
you got a little cucumber, or something. However. . . .'

The deputy turns to the constable with the tray, chooses
the least spoilt of all the apples and eats it.

'Oh . . . some of them aren't all that rotten!' says the
police inspector in a seemingly surprised tone of voice. 'Let's
have them here. I'll choose some too! Just put the tray here.
. . . The better ones we'll take out and peel, and you can
destroy the others. Anikita Nikolaich, let's have another
drink! We really ought to get together a bit more often and
discuss things. As it is, we just live on in these backwoods—
no education in these parts, no club, no decent company—
might as well be Australia! Come on now, pour out some

more! Doctor, have some apples! I've peeled them for you with my own fair hands!'

'Where would you like me to put the tray, sir?' the constable asks the police inspector who is leaving the cellar with the rest of the company.

'Tr-tray? What tray? Oh, I see! Destroy it together with the apples. . . . Because it's contagious.'

'You have eaten the apples, sir.'

'Oh . . . excellent! Look . . . you go over to my house and tell my wife not to be angry. . . . I'll only go off for an hour or so . . . to Plyunin's, to get some sleep. . . . Do you understand? Sleep . . . in the arms of Morpheus. Tra-la-la.'

And raising his eyes to heaven, the police inspector shakes his head bitterly, spreads out his hands and says:

'And that's the way our life goes!'

THE BOA-CONSTRICTOR AND THE
RABBIT

❋

PYOTR SEMYONYCH, a bedraggled, bald-headed individual
in a velvet dressing-gown with crimson tassels, stroked his
fluffy whiskers and continued:

'Well, mon cher, if you like there is one other method.
This is the subtlest, cleverest, most cunning method—and the
most dangerous one for husbands. It can only be understood
by psychologists and connoisseurs of the female heart. It has
a *conditio sine qua non:* patience, patience, and patience. If
a man doesn't know how to wait and be patient, then this
method is not for him. According to it, in order to seduce
somebody else's wife you keep as far away from her as
possible. When you feel madly attracted to her you cease
visiting her, you meet her as rarely as possible, and then
only for a moment, while at the same time denying yourself
the pleasure of talking to her. When using this method you
operate at a distance. The whole thing is a kind of hypnotism.
She must not see, but must feel you, like a rabbit feels the
gaze of the boa-constrictor. You hypnotise her not by your
gaze, but by the poison of your tongue, and the husband can
serve as the best transmission wire for this.

'For example, I'm in love with a certain N.N. and want
to seduce her. Somewhere in the club or at the theatre I meet
her husband.

' "And how's your wife?" I ask him in passing. "A most
charming woman, I must say. I like her awfully! In fact, I
like her a hell of a lot."

' "Mm. . . . What is it you like so much about her?"
asks the husband, very pleased.

' "She's a most delightful, romantic creature, who could even move a stone and make it fall in love with her! Incidentally, you husbands are prosaic people, and you only understand your wives during the first month of marriage. . . . Take it from me, your wife is an absolutely ideal woman! Take it from me, and rejoice that Fate has sent you such a wife! Women like that are precisely what we need in these times . . . just like that!"

' "Why, what is there so very special about her?" says the husband, surprised.

' "Good heavens! Why, she's a beauty, full of grace, life and truth, romantic, sincere and yet mysterious! Once women like that fall in love, they love violently, passionately. . . ."

'And more in the same strain. That very same day, when he is going to bed, the husband can't refrain from telling his wife:

' "I saw Pyotr Semyonych to-day. He praised you up to the skies! Was in ecstasies. . . . You're a beauty, and graceful, and mysterious . . . and apparently you're capable of loving in some special way. He really let himself go. . . . Ha-ha!"

'After that, without having seen *her*, I try to meet the husband again.

' "By the by, old boy . . ." I say to him. "A painter dropped in to see me yesterday. He's had a commission for two thousand roubles from some prince or other to paint the portrait of a typical Russian beauty. Asked me to look for a model for him. I'd have liked to send him to your wife, but felt shy about doing so. But your wife would be just right for it! She has a charming little head! I think it's a damned shame that no artist will ever see such a marvellous model. A damned shame!"

'One would have to be a terribly unkind husband not to pass that on to one's wife. Next morning his wife looks at the mirror for a long time and thinks:

' "What makes him think that I've got a typically Russian face?"

'After that she thinks of me every time she looks in the mirror. Meanwhile, my chance meetings with her husband continue. After one such meeting the husband comes home and begins peering at his wife's face.

' "What are you looking at me like that for?" she asks.

' "Why, that queer chap Pyotr Semyonych says you have one eye darker than the other. For the life of me, I can't see it!"

'His wife goes to the mirror again. She looks at herself for a long time, and thinks:

' "Yes, I think the left eye is a little darker than the right one. . . . No, I think the right one is darker than the left . . . but then it may just have seemed like that to him!"

'After the eighth or ninth meeting the husband says to his wife:

' "I saw Pyotr Semyonych at the theatre. He apologised for never coming to see you: he has no time! He says he's very busy. I don't think he's been to see us for about four months. . . . I began to haul him over the coals for it, but he apologised and said that he wouldn't come to see us until he'd finished some work or other."

' "Well, and when will he finish it?" asks his wife.

' "Not for a year or two, he says. But what kind of work that beggar can be doing, I'm damned if I know. He is a queer chap, honestly! Kept on at me for hours: Why doesn't your wife go on the stage? With such an attractive appearance, he says, with such intelligence and ability to feel, it's a sin to stay at home. She should give up everything, he says, and go where her inner voice tells her. Worldly limitations were not made for the likes of her. Natures like hers, he says, must stand outside time and space."

'His wife, of course, only dimly understands this harangue, but melts and is transported with delight all the same.

' "What nonsense!" she says, trying to appear indifferent. "And what else did he say?"

' "If I wasn't so busy, he says, I'd take her away from you. Well, go on, I says, take her—I shan't fight you for her. You

don't understand her, he shouts! She must be understood!
She has an exceptional nature, he says, a powerful one,
searching for an outlet! I'm sorry that I'm not Turgenev,
he says, or I'd have written about her long ago! Ha-ha! . . .
You've certainly made an impression on him! Well, old
fellow, I thought, you should live with her for a year or two,
then you'd change your tune. . . . He is a queer chap!"

'And his poor wife is gradually overwhelmed by a passionate desire to meet me. I am the only man who has understood
her, and there is so much she could say only to me! But I
persevere in not going to see her or running into her. She
has not seen me for a long time, but my excruciatingly sweet
poison has already infected her. Her husband transmits my
words to her with a yawn, but she feels that she hears my
voice and sees my shining eyes.

'The time has come to seize my chance. One evening her
husband comes home and says:

' "I've just seen Pyotr Semyonych. He seemed dull and
sad—crestfallen."

' "Why? What's the matter with him?"

' "Can't make it out. He complains that he's sunk in
melancholy. I'm lonely, he says; I haven't anyone close to
me, no friends, no kindred spirit who would understand me
and blend with my spirit. No one understands me, he says,
and now there's only one thing I want: death. . . ."

' "What nonsense!" his wife says, but she thinks to herself:
"Poor thing! I understand him perfectly! I'm lonely too,
no one understands me except him, so who could understand his state of mind better than I?"

' "Yes, he really is a queer chap . . ." the husband
continues. "I feel so sad, he says, I don't even go home; I
just walk up and down the N—— Boulevard all night.

'His wife is all in a fever. She passionately wants to go
to the N—— Boulevard and have a look—if only out of the
corner of her eye—at the man who has contrived to understand her and who is now sunk in melancholy. Who knows?

If she were to talk to him now, say a few words of consolation to him, perhaps he would stop suffering. If she were to tell him that he has a friend who understands and values him, he might rise again spiritually.

' "But it's impossible . . . mad," she thinks. "I shouldn't even think of it. I might fall in love with him if I'm not careful, but this is fantastic . . . stupid. . . ."

'When her husband finally falls asleep, she raises her feverish head, puts her finger to her lips, and thinks: What if she takes the risk of leaving the house now? Afterwards she can always concoct some story or other, say that she ran round to the chemist or the dentist.

' "I'll go!" she decides.

'She already has a plan prepared: she will leave the house by the back stairs, go to the boulevard in a cab, once there she will walk past him, have a look at him, and then go home. In that way she will compromise neither her husband nor herself.

'And she gets dressed, quietly leaves the house, and hurries to the boulevard. The boulevard is dark and deserted. The bare trees are sleeping. There is no one there. But then she sees someone's silhouette. That must be him. Trembling all over, oblivious of everything, she approaches me slowly . . . and I approach her. For a minute we stand in silence, looking into each other's eyes. Another minute passes in silence and . . . the rabbit falls defencelessly into the jaws of the boa-constrictor.'

HISTORY OF A BUSINESS ENTERPRISE

※

ANDREI ANDREICH SIDOROV inherited four thousand
roubles from his mother, and decided to open a bookshop with
the money. Now there was a great need for such a shop. The
town was stagnating in ignorance and prejudice; old men
did nothing but go to the public baths, civil servants played
cards and swilled vodka, ladies gossiped, young men lived
without any ideals, young girls dreamed of marriage all day
long and ate buckwheat porridge, husbands beat their
wives, and pigs wandered about the streets.

We need ideas, more ideas! thought Andrei Andreich. Ideas!

When he had rented the necessary premises he went to
Moscow, whence he returned with a great many books, both
classical and the most modern authors, and a great many
text books, and he arranged all that stuff on the shelves. Not
a single customer came in the course of the first three weeks.
Andrei Andreich sat behind the counter reading Mikhailovski*
and trying to think honestly. For example, when it would
suddenly occur to him that it would not be a bad idea to have
some bream with gruel to eat, he would immediately catch
himself out: 'Oh, how trivial!' he would say to himself.

Every morning a servant-girl chilled with cold, wearing
a kerchief and with leather galoshes on her bare feet, would
rush headlong into the shop and say:

'Give us two copecks' worth of vinegar!'

And Andrei Andreich would answer her disdainfully:

'You've mistaken the door, madam! You've come to the
wrong place, madam!'

* A writer of advanced political views. (*Translators' Note.*)

When one of his friends came to see him he would put on an important and mysterious expression, reach for the third volume of Pisarev* from the highest shelf, blow the dust off it and, with a look as if he had something else as well in the shop but was afraid to show it, he would say:

'Yes, sir, this little piece is so to speak . . . well, I mean in fact. . . . You read it, it would make you sit up all right . . . m-m-m. . . .'

'Look out you don't get it in the neck for reading it, old man!'

Three weeks passed before the first customer came. He was a fat, grey-haired gentleman with side-whiskers, and wearing a cap with a red band round it—by all appearances, a landowner. He demanded the second part of *Our Native Tongue*.

'You haven't any slate pencils?' he asked.

'I don't keep them.'

'Pity. . . . It's a bore to have to go to the bazaar for a little thing like that.'

It really is a pity that I don't keep slate pencils, thought Andrei Andreich when the customer had left. It's no use specialising too narrowly here in the provinces, one should sell everything that has anything to do with education and which promotes it in one way or another.

He wrote to Moscow, and before a month was out pens, pencils, penholders, school exercise books, slates and other school materials were displayed in his window. Boys and girls began dropping in from time to time, and there even came a day when his takings were one rouble, forty copecks. One day the servant girl in leather galoshes rushed headlong into the shop; he had already opened his mouth to tell her disdainfully that she had come to the wrong place, when she shouted:

'Give us a copeck's worth of paper and a seven copeck stamp!'

After that Andrei Andreich began keeping stamps, as well as application forms. About eight months after the opening of the shop a lady came in to buy pens.

* A writer of advanced political views. (*Translators' note.*)

'You don't happen to have any school satchels?' she asked.

'Alas, madam, I don't keep them!'

'Oh, what a pity! In that case, show me what dolls you have, only they mustn't be expensive. . . .'

'I haven't any dolls either, madam!' said Andrei Andreich sadly.

Without further ado he wrote to Moscow, and soon satchels, dolls, drums, swords, accordions, balls, and all sorts of toys appeared in his shop.

'Those are all trifles!' he said to his friends. 'But just you wait, I'll introduce educational toys and instructive games! You see, in my shop the educational section will be founded, as the saying goes, on the subtlest deductions of science, in short. . . .'

He ordered dumb-bells, croquet, backgammon, bagatelle, gardening tools for children, and about two dozen very clever, instructional games. Then, to their great delight, the inhabitants of the town saw, as they passed his shop, two bicycles, one large, and the other slightly smaller. And business went with a swing. Business was especially good before Christmas, when Andrei Andreich hung a notice in the window that he had Christmas tree decorations for sale.

'You'll see, I'll get hygiene across to them yet,' he said to his friends, rubbing his hands. 'Just you let me get to Moscow! I'll have such filters and all kinds of scientific improvements as in fact you've never dreamed of! Science can't be ignored, my friends, no-o-o!'

Having made a lot of money, he went to Moscow and bought—for cash and on credit—about five thousand roubles' worth of goods. There were filters, and excellent lamps for writing-tables, and guitars, and hygienic underpants for children, and feeding-bottles, and purses, and zoological collections. While he was about it he bought five hundred roubles' worth of best-quality china, and was glad that he had done so, as beautiful things develop refined taste and make for gentler manners. On his return from Moscow he set about arranging the new goods on the shelves and book-cases. Somehow it so happened that as he climbed up to tidy the top shelf something shook, and one after another the ten volumes of Mikhailovski fell off the shelf; one volume hit him on the head, the others fell down right on the lamps, and broke two lamp-globes.

'How . . . heavily they do write!' muttered Andrei Andreich, rubbing himself.

He collected all the books together, tied them up firmly with string, and hid them under the counter. About two days later he was told that his neighbour the grocer had been sentenced to hard labour for assaulting his nephew, and therefore the shop was to let. Andrei Andreich was very pleased, and asked if he could have the first refusal for it. A door was soon made in the wall, and both shops, joined into one, were filled up with goods; as the customers who went into the second half of the shop all asked for tea, sugar and kerosene from habit, Andrei Andreich without more ado introduced groceries as well.

He is now one of the most prominent shop-keepers in our town. He sells china, tobacco, tar, soap, bread-rolls, red wine, haberdashery and chandlery, rifles, skins and ham. He has taken over a wine-cellar in the market and, it is rumoured, is going to open public baths and a hotel. As to the books which once lay on his shelves, they—including the third volume of Pisarev—have long ago been sold for one rouble, five copecks the hundredweight.

At name-day parties and weddings his former friends, whom Andrei Andreich now calls 'Americans' in derision, sometimes bring the conversation round to progress, literature and other elevated subjects.

'Andrei Andreich, have you read the last number of the *European Herald?*' they ask him.

'No, I haven't read it . . .' he replies, screwing up his eyes and playing with his thick watch-chain. 'That doesn't concern us. We are occupied with more constructive business.'

75,000

❉

ONE night, at about midnight, two friends were walking along the Tverskoi Boulevard. One was tall, dark and handsome, dressed in a shabby bear-skin coat and a top hat, the other—a small, red-haired man wearing a rust-coloured coat with white bone buttons. They both walked in silence. The man with the dark hair was faintly whistling a mazurka, the red-haired man was looking at his feet and frequently spitting to the side.

'Shall we sit down?' proposed the dark-haired man at last, when both friends saw the sombre silhouette of Pushkin's monument and the little light over the gates of the Strastnoi monastery.

The red-haired man silently agreed, and the friends sat down.

'I've got a little request to make of you, Nikolai Borisych,' said the man with dark hair after a short silence. 'Could you lend me ten or fifteen roubles, old man? I'll pay you back in a week's time. . . .'

The red-haired man was silent.

'I wouldn't have bothered you if it wasn't a dire necessity. Fate played a rotten trick on me today. . . . This morning my wife gave me her bracelet to pawn. . . . She has to pay for her little sister at school. Well, I pawned it and then. . . . I lost the money at cards quite accidentally, when you were with me today. . . .'

The red-haired man stirred and grunted.

'You're a poor fish, Vasili Ivanovich!' he said, and a malicious sneer spread over his mouth. 'A poor fish! What right had you to sit and play cards with ladies if you knew that it was not your money, but someone else's? Well, aren't you a poor fish, aren't you a fop? Wait, don't interrupt. . . . Let me give you a piece of my mind, once and for all. . . . What are all these eternal new suits for, that tie-pin there? Is fashion for paupers like you? What's that idiotic top-hat for? You, living on your wife, pay fifteen roubles for a top-hat when, without doing any harm to fashion or taste, you could very well go about in a three-rouble cap! Why all this boasting about non-existent friendships? You know Khokhlov and Plevako and all the editors! When you were lying about your friends today my eyes and ears were burning for you! You lie and don't even blush! And when you play with those women, lose your wife's money to them, you smile in such a trite and stupid way that . . . you make one feel that you aren't even worth a slap in the face!'

'Oh, drop it, drop it. . . . You're out of sorts to-day. . . .'

'Well, let's say that your foppishness is all due to youth, that you're merely behaving like a school-boy. . . . I'm ready to admit that, Vasili Ivanovich . . . you're still young. . . . But I won't admit . . . there's one thing I don't understand. . . . How could you cheat when you were playing with those dolls? . . . When you were dealing, I saw you give yourself the ace of spades from underneath!'

Vasili Ivanovich blushed like a school-boy and began to justify himself. The red-haired man stood his ground. They quarrelled loud and long. At last they both became silent, plunged in thought.

'It's true, I have got into an awful mess,' said the man with dark hair after a long silence. 'It's true. . . . I've spent everything, run into debt, used a bit of other people's money, and now I don't know how to extricate myself. Do you know that unbearable, awful feeling when your whole body itches, and you can't do anything about it? That's rather like the feeling I'm experiencing now. . . . I'm entangled up to my ears. . . . I'm ashamed of myself, and ashamed of other

people's opinion. . . . I do masses of stupid and disgusting
things for the pettiest of reasons, and at the same time I
simply can't stop myself. . . . It's awful! If I was to inherit
or win some money, I'd give up everything in the world, I
believe, and be born anew. . . . But don't pass judgment on
me, Nikolai Borisych . . . don't throw the first stone. . . .
Remember Palmov's Neklyujev.'

'I do remember your Neklyujev,' said the red-haired man.
'I remember. . . . He gobbled up other people's money,
gorged himself, and then wanted to have some after-dinner
relaxation: he went and snivelled to a flapper. He was
careful not to snivel before dinner. . . . Authors should be
ashamed of idealising rotters like that. If Neklyujev hadn't
had an attractive appearance and a gallant way with him,
a rich man's daughter wouldn't have fallen in love with him
and there wouldn't have been any regrets. . . . In general,
fate gives rotters an attractive appearance. . . . Why, you're
all cupids! They love you, they fall in love with you. . . .
You're frightfully lucky so far as women are concerned!'

The red-haired man stood up and walked round the bench.

'Now, take your wife, for example . . . an honest, noble-
minded woman . . . what could have made her fall in love
with you? What? And today, the whole evening while you
were lying and putting on airs, a pretty blonde couldn't take
her eyes off you. . . . They love you, you Neklyujevs, offer
themselves to you—whereas one works all one's life, struggles
like mad . . . as honest as honesty itself, and—if only one
had one moment of happiness! What's more . . . do you
remember? I was engaged to your wife Olga Alexeyevna
before she met you, I was happy for a little, but you turned
up, and . . . I was done for.'

'Jealousy!' laughed the man with dark hair. 'Why, I
didn't know you were so jealous!'

A look of annoyance and repulsion passed over Nikolai
Borisych's face. . . . He stretched his hand out mechanically, without realising what he was doing . . . and made a

gesture. The sound of a slap broke the silence of the night.
. . . The top-hat flew off the dark-haired man's head and
rolled on the trodden snow. All this happened in a second,
unexpectedly, and was stupid and ridiculous. The red-haired
man immediately felt ashamed of his slap. He buried his face
in the collar of his coat and strode off along the boulevard.
When he reached Pushkin he looked round at the man with
dark hair, stood motionless for a minute, and then, just as if
he was frightened of something, he ran in the direction of
Tverskaya Street. . . .

Vasili Ivanovich sat on for a long time in silence. He never
moved. Some woman walked past him and, with a laugh,
handed him his top-hat. He thanked her mechanically,
stood up, and walked away.

Now for the nagging, he thought, half an hour later, as
he climbed the long staircase to his flat. . . . I'll catch it
from my spouse for losing! She'll preach at me all night!
To hell with her! I'll say that I mislaid the money. . . .

He reached his door, and rang timidly. The cook let him in.

'Congratulations!' the cook said to him, grinning all over
her face.

'Why?'

'You'll see, sir. God has been good to you!'

Vasili Ivanovich shrugged his shoulders and went into the
bed-room. There at the writing-table sat his wife, Olga
Alexeyevna, a small blonde with her hair in curlers. She was
writing. Before her lay several letters, already written and
sealed. When she saw her husband she jumped up and threw
her arms around his neck.

'You've come!' she said. 'What luck! You can't imagine
what luck! It was such a surprise that I had hysterics,
Vasya. . . . Here, read this!'

She jumped up, picked up the newspaper from the table,
and thrust it in her husband's face.

'Read it! My lottery ticket has won 75,000 roubles! I have
got a ticket, you know! Honestly I have! I hid it from you

because . . . because . . . you would have pawned it.
Nikolai Borisych gave me this ticket when I was engaged to
him, and then afterwards he didn't want to take it back.
What a good man Nikolai Borisych is! Now we're frightfully
rich! Now you'll turn over a new leaf, you won't lead a
dissolute life. Why, you went out on the spree and deceived
me because you were in need, you were poor. I understand
that. You're intelligent, decent. . . .'

She paced up and down the room and laughed.

'It was a surprise! I was walking up and down the room
and cursing you for your dissoluteness, hating you, and then I
sat down to read the paper out of sheer boredom. . . . And
suddenly I saw it! . . . I've written letters to everyone . . .
to my sisters, to my mother. . . . How pleased they'll be,
poor things! But where are you going to?'

Vasili Ivanovich had a look at the paper. . . . Stunned,
pale, not listening to his wife, he stood for some time in
silence, thinking something out, then put on his top-hat and
left the house.

'To Number NN, Bolshaya Dmitrovka!' he shouted to the
cabby.

He did not find the person he wanted in the hotel. The
room which he knew, was locked.

She must be at the theatre, he thought: and after the
theatre she went to have supper somewhere. . . . I'll wait
a little.

And he remained there, waiting. . . . Half an hour
passed, an hour. . . . He walked down the corridor and
chatted to a sleepy servant. . . . Downstairs the clock in the
hotel hall struck three. . . . Finally, he lost patience and
began slowly to go down the stairs to the exit. . . . But Fate
took pity on him. . . .

At the very entrance he met a tall, brown-haired,
emaciated woman wrapped up in a long boa. Close on her
heels followed a gentleman wearing dark glasses and an
astrakhan cap.

5

'Excuse me,' Vasili Ivanovich addressed the lady. 'Could I trouble you for a moment?'

The lady and gentleman frowned.

'I won't be a moment,' the lady said to the man, and went with Vasili Ivanovich towards the gas-bracket. . . . 'What do you want?'

'I've come to see you . . . on business, Nadine,' began Vasili Ivanovich, stuttering. . . . 'It's a pity you've got that gentleman with you, or I'd tell you all about it. . . .'

'Well, what is it? I'm in a hurry!'

'You've got yourself some new admirers, so you're in a hurry! You're a fine one, I must say! Why did you send me packing at Christmas time? You didn't want to live with me because . . . because I didn't supply you with sufficient means of existence. . . . Well, it turns out that you were wrong. . . . Yes. . . . Do you remember that ticket I gave you on your name-day? Well, read this! It's won 75,000 roubles!'

The lady took the newspaper in her hands, and with greedy, almost frightened eyes she began to search for the telegram from Petersburg. . . . And she found it. . . .

At that very same time, other eyes, red with tears and dulled by grief, almost crazy, were looking for the ticket in a casket. . . . Those eyes searched for it all night, and did not find it. The ticket had been stolen, and Olga Alexeyevna knew who had stolen it.

That same night red-haired Nikolai Borisych was tossing from side to side and trying to fall asleep, but he did not do so before morning. He was ashamed of that slap.

THE MASK

❋

A FANCY-DRESS ball or—as the local ladies called it—a
bal paré, was being given in aid of charity in the Social Club
at X——.

It was midnight. The non-dancing intelligentsia—there
were five of them—who were not wearing masks, were
sitting round a big table in the reading-room and, with their
noses and beards buried in newspapers, were reading,
snoozing and, as the local correspondent of the metropolitan
papers—a gentleman of very advanced ideas—expressed it,
cogitating.

Strains of the quadrille 'Vyushka' reached them from the
main ballroom. Waiters kept on running past the door,
stamping their feet loudly and clattering crockery. In the
reading-room itself deep silence reigned.

'I think it'll be more comfortable in here!' a low, slightly
smothered voice which seemed to be coming from the stove
was suddenly heard to say. 'Hop in here! This way, kids!'

The door opened, and into the reading-room came a
broad, thickset man dressed in a coachman's costume and a
hat with peacock feather in it, and wearing a mask. Behind
him came two ladies in masks and a waiter with a tray.
On the tray was a fat bottle containing liqueur, about three
bottles of red wine, and some glasses.

'This way! It'll be cooler in here,' the man said. 'Put the
tray on the table. . . . Sit down, mardemoselles! Je vous
prie à la trimonrin. And you move up, gentlemen . . . and
look sharp!'

The man swayed and swept some magazines from the
table with his hand.

'Put it here! And you, you readers, move up; this isn't the time for newspapers and politics. . . . Drop it!'

'Would you mind being a little quieter, please,' said one of the intellectuals, looking at the mask through his glasses. 'This is the reading-room, not the bar. . . . You can't drink here.'

'Why can't I drink here? Does the table rock, or is the ceiling likely to fall in? Odd! But . . . I've no time for conversation! Drop those newspapers. . . . You've read a bit, and that's enough; you're very clever as it is anyway, and what's more you'll spoil your eyes, but most important of all—I don't want it, and that's that.'

The waiter had put the tray on the table, and stood at the door with a table-napkin over his arm. The ladies at once set to work on the red wine.

'How clever these people must be to like their newspapers better than these drinks . . .' the man with the peacock feathers began to say, pouring himself out a liqueur, 'But in my opinion you, my dear sirs, like your newspapers because you haven't anything to buy drinks with. Am I right? Ha-ha! Reading! Well, what do they write about? You, gentleman in the glasses! What are you reading about? Ha-ha! Go on, drop it! Go on, don't be difficult! Better have a drink!'

The man with the peacock feathers got up and snatched the newspaper out of the hands of the gentleman in glasses. The latter grew pale, then blushed and looked in amazement at the other intellectuals—and they at him.

'You're forgetting yourself, sir!' he spluttered. 'You are turning the reading-room into a public house, you make so bold as to behave rowdily, snatch newspapers out of people's hands! I won't allow it! You don't know who you're dealing with, my dear sir. I'm Jestyakov, the bank manager!'

'I don't care a damn whether you're Jestyakov or not! And as to your newspaper—that's what it's good for. . . .'

The man picked up the newspaper and tore it into scraps.

'Gentlemen, what is this?' stammered Jestyakov in stupefaction. 'It's odd, it . . . it's almost supernatural. . . .'

'They're getting waxy . . .' laughed the man. 'Fie, fie! You're in a funk! You're shaking in your shoes! That's how it is, my dear sirs! But jokes apart, I'm not keen on chatting with you. . . . Because I want to be alone with mardemoselles, and because I want to have some fun and games here, I would ask you not to counterdict, but to go away. . . . If you please, gentlemen! Mr. Belebukhin, go to the devil! Why are you wrinkling your snout like that? I said get out, so get out! You'd better look sharp, or you'll get a kick in the pants if you're unlucky!'

'What is this?' asked Belebukhin, treasurer to the Orphans' Trust, blushing and shrugging his shoulders. 'I can't even understand it. . . . Some cad or other bursts in here and . . . suddenly starts saying things like that!'

'What was that word—cad?' shouted the man with the peacock feathers, getting angry, and he hit the table with his fist so that the glasses jumped on the tray. 'Who are you speaking to? Do you think that because I am wearing a mask you can call me names? You spitfire, you! Get out, when I tell you. Bank manager, get out while the going's good! Get out, all of you, I don't want any of you swine here! Get along, go to hell!'

'We'll just see!' said Jestyakov, whose very glasses were sweating from agitation. 'I'll show you! Hey, tell the club steward on duty to come here!'

A moment later a small red-haired steward wearing a blue ribbon in his lapel came into the room, out of breath from dancing.

'Would you please go out of here!' he began. 'This isn't the place to drink. Please go to the bar!'

'Where did you spring from?' asked the man in the mask. 'Did I send for you?'

'Please don't be familiar, and leave the room!'

'Look here, my good man: I'll give you one more minute.

. . . As you're the steward, and the chief person here, just you take these chaps by the arm and lead them out. My mesdemoiselles don't like it if there are strangers here. . . . They're shy, and I want them in a natural state so as to get my money's worth.'

'This preposterous autocrat obviously doesn't realise that this isn't a pig-sty,' shouted Jestyakov. 'Ask Evstrat Spiridonych to come here!'

'Evstrat Spiridonych!' resounded through the club. 'Where is Evstrat Spiridonych?'

Evstrat Spiridonych, an old man in a police officer's uniform, was not slow in appearing.

'Would you please leave!' he croaked, his awe-inspiring eyes protruding and his moustache bristling.

'Why, he really frightened me!' said the man, and roared with laughter from sheer delight. 'Honest to God, he did! What terrifying things one does see, strike me pink! Whiskers like a cat, eyes popping out. . . . Ha, ha, ha!'

'I'd ask you not to argue!' Evstrat Spiridonych shouted with all his strength, trembling. 'Get out! I'll have you thrown out!'

An inconceivable noise arose in the reading-room. Evstrat Spiridonych, as red as a lobster, shouted and stamped his feet. Jestyakov shouted. Belebukhin shouted. All the intellectuals shouted, but all their voices were drowned by the low, thick, slightly smothered bass of the man in the mask. Owing to the general confusion the dancing had stopped, and the public poured from the ballroom into the reading-room.

Evstrat Spiridonych, so as to look imposing, summoned all the police officers who were in the club, and sat down to write a report.

'Go on, write, write,' said the masked man, prodding at the pen with his finger. 'What will become of me now, poor thing? Poor little hothead! What are you ruining me for—and me a poor little orphan! Ha-ha! Well? Is the report ready? You've all signed? Well, now have a look! One . . . two . . . three. . . !'

The man stood up, stretched to his full height, and tore off his mask. Having uncovered his drunken face and looked at everyone, admiring the effect he had produced, he fell into an armchair and guffawed joyfully. And he had, indeed, made an extraordinary impression. All the intellectuals looked at each other in embarrassment and turned pale, some of them scratched the backs of their heads. Evstrat Spiridonych groaned like a man who had unexpectedly done something extremely foolish.

They had all recognised that the ruffian was the local millionaire, a manufacturer called Pyatigorov, a 'Honorary Citizen' who was well-known for his scandalous behaviour, for his philanthropy and, as the local paper had more than once remarked, for his love of enlightenment.

'Well, will you go away or won't you?' asked Pyatigorov after a moment's silence.

The intellectuals went out of the room on tiptoe, without saying a word. Pyatigorov closed the door behind them.

'But you knew it was Pyatigorov!' croaked Evstrat Spiridonych in an undertone a moment later, shaking the shoulder of the waiter who had taken the wine into the reading-room. 'Why didn't you say so?'

'He told me not to, sir.'

'Told me not to! I'll put you in jug for a month, damn you. I'll give you "told me not to". Get out!! And you're fine ones, gentlemen,' he turned to the intellectuals. 'You started a riot! You couldn't even go out of the reading-room for five minutes! You've made your bed, now you must lie on it. Oh, gentlemen, gentlemen! I don't like the look of it, I really don't!'

The intellectuals went about the club despondent, lost, guilty, whispering to each other, behaving as if they had a premonition of something unpleasant. Their wives and daughters, when they learnt that Pyatigorov was 'offended' and cross, fell silent and began going home. The dancing stopped.

At two o'clock Pyatigorov came out of the reading-room; he was drunk and walked unsteadily. He went into the ball-room, sat down near the orchestra, and dozed off, lulled by the music; then his head drooped sadly, and he gave a snore.

'Stop playing!' the stewards made signs at the musicians. 'Sh! Yegor Nilich is asleep. . . .'

'Wouldn't you like me to take you home, Yegor Nilich?' asked Belebukhin, bending down to the millionaire's ear.

Pyatigorov pursed his lips exactly as if he wanted to blow a fly off his cheek.

'Wouldn't you like me to take you home?' Belebukhin repeated, 'or order the carriage?'

'Eh? Who? You . . . what d'you want?'

'To take you home, sir. It's time for bye-byes. . . .'

'I w-want to go home. . . . T-take me!'

Belebukhin beamed with pleasure and began lifting Pyatigorov up. The other intellectuals jumped to help him and, smiling pleasantly, they lifted the 'Honorary Citizen' up and carefully carried him to the carriage.

'Why, only an artist, someone with talent, can fool a whole party like that,' said Jestyakov gaily as he helped him into his seat. 'I'm really amazed, Yegor Nilich! I'm still laughing about it . . . ha-ha! And there we were, getting worked up and making a fuss! Ha-ha! Would you believe it? I've never laughed so much even in the theatre. . . . A wealth of humour! I shall remember this memorable evening all my life!'

When they had taken Pyatigorov home the intellectuals cheered up and became calmer.

'He shook my hand when we said good-bye,' said Jestyakov, very pleased. 'So it's all right, he's not angry. . . .'

'Please God!' sighed Evstrat Spiridonych. 'He's a scoundrel, a despicable fellow, but still—a benefactor! . . . One can't treat him like that! . . .'

AN UNPLEASANT INCIDENT

❧

THE district doctor, Grigori Ivanovich Ovchinnikov, aged about thirty-five, a thin, highly-strung man known to his colleagues for his short treatises on Medical Statistics and his passionate interest in so-called 'social problems', was going round the wards in his hospital one morning. He was, as usual, followed by the male nurse, Mikhail Zakharovich, a middle-aged man with an oily face, lanky, greasy hair and an ear-ring in one ear.

The doctor had only just started on his rounds when a trifling matter aroused his suspicions. It was the following: the male nurse's waistcoat kept wrinkling itself into creases and stubbornly rucking itself up in spite of the fact that the nurse was constantly smoothing it down and adjusting it. The male nurse's shirt was also all crumpled and rucked up. White down was sticking here and there to his long, black frock-coat, to his trousers and even to his tie. Obviously the nurse had slept all night without undressing and to judge by the expression with which he was now smoothing down his waistcoat and adjusting his tie, he felt uncomfortable in his clothes.

The doctor had a close look at him and saw what the matter was. The male nurse did not sway and he answered questions coherently, but his dull and sullen face, his bleary eyes, the gooseflesh on his neck and shaking hands, the disorder in his dress, and above all the strenuous efforts he was making to master himself, and his desire to camouflage his real condition were witnesses to the fact that he had only just got up from bed, that he had not had enough sleep and that he was drunk, very drunk still from the night before.

He was in the throes of the painful after-effects of drink and was suffering and very dissatisfied with himself.

The doctor, who did not like his male nurse for reasons of his own, felt a strong desire to say to him: 'I see you are drunk!' The waistcoat, the long-skirted frock-coat, the ear-ring in the fleshy ear suddenly filled him with disgust, but he restrained this unkind feeling and said softly and politely, as always:

'Have you given Gerasim his milk?'

'I have, sir,' answered Mikhail Zakharovich also softly.

As he was talking to the patient, Gerasim, the doctor glanced at the temperature chart, and feeling a new wave of loathing mounting up, held his breath so as not to speak, but could not restrain himself and asked gruffly, in a choking voice:

'Why isn't the temperature entered on the chart?'

'Oh, yes it is, sir!' said Mikhail Zakharovich softly, but having looked at the chart and convinced himself that the temperature had not, in fact, been entered on it, he shrugged his shoulders in embarrassment and muttered, 'I don't know, it's probably Nadejda Osipovna's fault.'

'Last night's is not entered either!' continued the doctor. 'All you care about is getting drunk, damn you! Even now you are as drunk as a coot! Where is Nadejda Osipovna?'

Nadejda Osipovna, the maternity nurse, was not in the wards, though she had to be present every morning when the dressings were changed. The doctor looked round and it seemed to him that the ward had not been cleaned, that it was untidy, that none of the things that ought to have been done had, in fact, been done and that everything was as rucked up, crumpled and covered with down as his male nurse's disgusting waistcoat—and he wanted to tear off his own white coat, swear, throw everything up, leave it and go. But he made an effort and continued on his rounds.

Gerasim was followed by a surgical case with inflammation of the cellular tissues in the right arm. He had to have a new dressing. The doctor sat down on a stool in front of him and busied himself with the arm.

That's all because they were celebrating someone's name day, . . . he thought, slowly taking off the dressing. You just wait, I'll show you name days! But actually, what can I do? Nothing at all.

He felt the abscess on the swollen, purple arm and said, 'A scalpel!'

Mikhail Zakharovich, in an attempt to show that he was firm on his legs, and fit for work, rushed off and quickly brought a scalpel.

'Not that one! Give me a new one,' said the doctor.

The male nurse trotted off to a chair on which was placed a box with the dressing material and began hurriedly rummaging in it. There was a lot of whispering between him and the maids, he kept shuffling the box on its chair, rustled something, dropped something twice, while the doctor sat, waited and felt his back itching with irritation as a result of the whispering and the rustling.

'Well, how long are you going to be?' he asked. 'You probably forgot them downstairs. . . .'

The male nurse came running up with two scalpels, but inadvertently breathed in the doctor's direction.

'They're the wrong ones!' said the doctor irritably. 'I'm telling you in plain Russian, give me the new ones. And anyway, go and have a sleep, you reek like a pub! You're not in your right mind!'

'What other knives do you want?' asked the male nurse irritably, and slowly shrugged his shoulders.

He was annoyed with himself and ashamed because the patients and the nurses were looking straight at him, and to show that he was not ashamed he gave a forced smile and repeated:

'What other knives do you want?'

The doctor felt tears in his eyes and his fingers shook. He made an effort and said in a trembling voice:

'Go and get yourself some sleep! I don't want to speak to a drunk.'

'You can only reprimand me on account of my work,' continued the male nurse, 'and if, say, I'm a bit drunk, no one has the right to tell me how to behave. I'm doing my work, aren't I? What else do you want? Aren't I doing my work?'

The doctor jumped up and without realising what he was doing he lifted his hand and slapped the male nurse's face with all his might. He did not understand what he was doing it for, but had a great feeling of satisfaction at the fact that his fist got the male nurse right in the face and that a respectable, sedate and pious family man, well aware of his own worth, had swayed, bounced like a ball and sat down on a stool. He had a passionate desire to strike once more, but on seeing the pale, worried faces of the maids near the hated face, the feeling of satisfaction left him, he made a gesture of annoyance and ran out of the ward.

In the courtyard he met Nadejda Osipovna, a girl of twenty-seven, with a pale-yellow face and loose hair, who was going to the hospital. Her pink cotton dress had a very tight skirt which made her take very many and very small steps. Her dress rustled and she shrugged her shoulders with every step she took and shook her head as if she was mentally singing a gay little tune.

Ah, the mermaid! thought the doctor, remembering that in the hospital the maternity nurse had been given the nickname of mermaid, and he was pleased at the thought that he would now tear a strip off that mincing, over-dressed woman who was so much in love with herself.

'Where have you been?' he shouted as he came up to her. 'Why aren't you in the hospital? The temperatures aren't charted, chaos everywhere, the male nurse is drunk, you sleep till twelve o'clock! . . . Please look for another job! You're not working here any more!'

When he reached his flat, the doctor tore off his white coat and the towel he had tied round his waist, threw them both angrily into a corner and began pacing up and down his study.

'God, what people, what people!' he muttered. 'Enemies of all work, that's what they are—they're not assistants! I can't work any more—I'm at the end of my tether. I'll leave!'

His heart was beating fast, he was trembling all over and wanted to weep; and to get rid of these feelings he began to soothe himself with the thought of how right he was and how well he had done to have struck the male nurse. To begin with, it was wrong, thought the doctor, that the male nurse should have obtained the job in the hospital not in the ordinary way but because he enjoyed the protection of his aunt who was nanny to the children of the Chairman of the Rural Council (it was disgusting to look at that influential aunt, behaving as if she was at home whenever she came to hospital for treatment and claiming to be received out of turn). The male nurse had but a slight idea of discipline, knew little and did not at all understand whatever he did know. He was never sober, he was impertinent and dirty, he took bribes from patients and sold the hospital drugs on the sly. Everyone knew, too, that he had his own practice, and treated the young men in town for secret ailments and, besides, used his own home-made remedies for the purpose. It wouldn't have been half so bad if he had merely been a quack of a kind of which there were many, but he was a convinced and an inwardly protesting quack. He cupped the out-patients and did blood-letting for them by stealth behind the doctor's back, was present at operations with his hands unwashed, always probed wounds with a dirty probe—this was enough to see how profound and sweeping was his contempt for medical science with all its learning and pedantry.

After waiting till his fingers no longer shook, the doctor

sat down at a table and wrote a letter to the Chairman of the Rural Council:

Dear Lev Trofimovich. Unless on receipt of this letter, your Council dismisses male nurse Smirnovski and grants me the right to choose my own male nurse, I shall feel compelled (not, of course, without regret) to ask you to consider me as being no longer doctor of N. hospital and to look for someone to take my place. Remember me to Lyubov Feodorovna and to Yus.

Yours sincerely,
G. Ovchinnikov.

The doctor re-read this letter and found it short and insufficiently cold. Besides, the request to remember him to Lyubov Feodorovna and Yus (such was the nickname of the Chairman's youngest son) was worse than out of place in an official business letter.

To hell with Yus! thought the doctor. He tore up the letter and began composing another:

Dear Sir, . . . he thought, sitting down at the open window and looking at the ducks and ducklings which tottered and stumbled as they hurried along the road, probably towards the pond; one duckling picked up on the road a length of pipe, choked and set up an anxious cheep; another ran up to it, seized the pipe out of its beak and also choked. . . . Some distance away, near the fence, where young lime trees were casting the lace-work of their shadows on the grass, Darya, the cook, was wandering round picking sorrel for green soup. . . . He could hear voices. . . . Zot, the coachman, with a bridle in his hand, and Manouilo, the hospital orderly, in a dirty white coat, were standing near a barn, talking about something and laughing.

That must be about my striking the male nurse, . . . thought the doctor. The whole county will know of this row by the evening. . . . Well then: Dear Sir, Unless your Council dismisses. . . .

The doctor knew perfectly well that the Rural Council would never choose his male nurse in preference to himself and would rather have no male nurse in the whole county than lose so excellent a man as Doctor Ovchinnikov. Probably, immediately on receipt of the letter Lev Trofimovich would arrive in his troika and start off: 'What's this ridiculous idea, old man? My dear fellow, what's all this about? Good God! Why? Whatever for? Where is he? Bring the beggar here! Sack him! We must sack him! He mustn't stay here another day, the old rascal!' After that, he would dine with the doctor, and after dinner he would lie down on that red sofa, stomach upwards, cover his face with a newspaper and snore; then having had his sleep, he would drink tea and depart taking the doctor with him for the night. And the whole affair would end with both the male nurse staying in the hospital and the doctor not tendering his resignation.

But in his heart of hearts the doctor wanted quite a different *dénoument*. He wanted the orderly's aunt to triumph and the Council to accept his resignation without further ado and even with pleasure, in spite of his eight years' conscientious service. He was dreaming of how he would leave the hospital to which he was used, of how he would write a letter to the magazine, *The Doctor*, of how his colleagues would present him with an address to show their sympathy for him. . . .

The mermaid appeared on the road. With her dress rustling and taking small steps, she came up to the window and asked:

'Grigori Ivanych, will you be receiving the patients yourself or do you want us to do it without you?'

But her eyes were saying: 'You lost your temper, but now you've calmed down and you feel ashamed, but I am magnanimous and take no notice of it.'

'All right, I'm coming in a minute,' said the doctor.

He again put on his white coat, girded himself with the towel and went to the hospital.

It was a bad thing to have run away after striking him, . . . he thought; as if I was embarrassed or frightened. . . . Behaved like a school-boy. . . . Very bad!

He thought that when he entered the ward the patients would be too embarrassed to look at him and that he would also feel ill at ease, but when he came in the patients were calmly lying in their beds and paid scarcely any attention to him. The face of Gerasim, the consumptive, expressed complete indifference and seemed to say: 'He did something to annoy you, you gave him a bit of a lesson. . . . Can't avoid that, old man.'

The doctor lanced two abscesses on the purple arm and put on a dressing, then went to the Women's Ward, where he operated on a woman's eye, and all the time he was being followed by the mermaid who helped him with an air as if nothing had happened and everything was fine. When he finished his round, he began the reception of out-patients. The window of the doctor's small consulting room was wide open. By merely sitting on the window-sill and stooping down a little, one could see young grass about a yard away. The previous evening there had been a thunderstorm accompanied by a heavy shower and the grass therefore looked a bit trampled and glossy. The path running past the window and towards the ravine appeared washed and the surgery's broken china, also washed and strewn on either side of it, gleamed in the sun and gave out rays of dazzling brilliance. And further away, on the other side of the path, young fir-trees, clad in rich, green dresses, pressed close to one another, and behind them stood the birches with their trunks as white as paper, and through the birches' green leaves lightly quivering in the wind, could be seen the bottomless blue sky. If one looked out of the window, the starlings hopping on the path would turn their stupid beaks towards the window and try to make up their minds whether to take fright or not. And having decided to do so, they would all, one after the other, rush off to the tops of the birches with a glad cry as if making fun of the doctor who was unable to fly.

The freshness and the fragrance of the spring day came through the heavy smell of iodine. It was good to breathe!

'Anna Spiridonova,' called the doctor.

A young peasant woman in a red dress entered the consulting room and made a short prayer to the Holy Image in the corner.

'Where's your pain?' asked the doctor.

The woman squinted mistrustfully at the door by which she had entered and at the door leading into the surgery, edged up to the doctor and whispered:

'No children!'

'Who else hasn't registered?' shouted the mermaid in the surgery. 'Come in and register!'

The very fact, thought the doctor as he was examining the woman, that he has made me use force for the first time in my life marks him out as a brute. Never in all my born days have I used force before.

Anna Spiridonova went. She was followed by an old man with a venereal disease, then a woman with three children who had a rash, and work came in with a rush. The male nurse failed to put in an appearance. Behind the surgery door the mermaid's dress was rustling, she was making a clanking noise with the various utensils and keeping up a cheerful twitter; she constantly came into the consulting room to help give treatment or take prescriptions, and did it all with an air to show that everything was all right.

She is pleased I struck the male nurse, thought the doctor, listening to the maternity nurse's voice. After all, they get on no better than a cat and dog, and it'll be a red-letter day for her if he is sacked. The nurses are pleased too, I think. . . . How awful it all is!

At the very height of the reception it began to seem to him that the maternity nurse and the other nurses and even the patients were deliberately trying to assume indifferent

6

and cheerful expressions. It was as if they understood that he was feeling ashamed and hurt, but were too considerate to show it. And he, wanting to prove to them that he was not at all ashamed, shouted angrily:

'Hullo, you there! Shut the door, there's a draught.'

But in truth he felt ashamed and had a heavy heart. He saw forty-five patients and left the hospital with slow and deliberate steps. The maternity nurse who had had time to go to her flat and put on a bright-red shawl over her shoulders, was now hurrying away somewhere, probably to a case or on a visit to friends; she had a cigarette between her lips and a flower in her hair which she wore loose. The patients were sitting on the threshold of the hospital and were silently warming themselves in the sun. The starlings were still making their noise and chasing the beetles. The doctor looked around him and thought that among all those even and quiet lives only two—the male nurse's and his own —stood out in sharp contrast and were as useless as broken keys in a piano. The male nurse was probably in bed trying to sleep off the effects of drink, but the thought that he had been in the wrong, had been insulted and had lost his job did not let him fall asleep. He was in a distressing situation. The doctor, on the other hand, never having struck anyone before, felt as if he had for ever lost his chastity. He was no longer accusing the male nurse or justifying himself; he was merely puzzled how it could have happened that he had struck someone—he, a decent man who had never even beaten a dog. When he had reached his flat he lay down on the sofa in his study, turned his head to the wall and began to meditate thus:

He is a bad man and does harm to our work; in the course of his three years' service my resentment has been gradually increasing, but nevertheless, nothing can justify my action. I have taken advantage of the fact that I am in the stronger position. He is my subordinate, is in the wrong and, besides, he is drunk, while I am his chief, am in the right and am sober. . . . In other words, I am in the stronger position.

Secondly, I struck him in the presence of people to whom I represent authority, and I have therefore given them a disgraceful example. . . .

The doctor was called in to dinner. . . . He ate a few spoonfuls of cabbage soup, got up from the table and lay down on the sofa again.

What shall I do now? he went on thinking. I must give him satisfaction as soon as possible. . . . But how? As a practical man he considers duels to be foolish, or doesn't understand them. If I should apologise to him in that same Ward and in the presence of nurses and patients, this apology would only satisfy me and not him; he is a bad man and would interpret my apology as cowardice or fear—fear that he will complain of me to the authorities. Besides, this apology of mine will completely ruin all hospital discipline. Should I offer him money? No, that is immoral and looks like bribery. If now, for the sake of argument, I should turn for the solution of the problem to our direct superiors, that is to the Rural Council. . . . It could officially reprimand me or dismiss me. . . . But it won't do that. Besides, it's a bit awkward, dragging the Council into the hospital's intimate internal concerns. And, anyway, it has no right to meddle in those things. . . .

About three hours after dinner the doctor, on his way to the pond for a bathe, was thinking:

Or should I do as everyone else does on these occasions? I mean, let him take legal action. I'm definitely the guilty party, I shall not try to defend myself and the Magistrate will give me a prison sentence. In this way the offended party will be satisfied and those who take me to represent authority will see that I was in the wrong.

He liked that idea. He was pleased and began to think that the problem was solved satisfactorily and that there could not be a more just solution.

Well then, that's excellent! he thought, as he got into the water and watched shoals of small, golden carp scuttling away in all directions—let him take legal action. . . . He can do it all the more easily as our official relationship is at an end and after this row one of us must leave the hospital anyway. . . .

In the evening the doctor ordered the gig to be made ready as he wanted to go to the District Military Commander for a game of vint.

He was quite ready and was standing in the middle of the study in his hat and coat, putting on his gloves, when the outside door opened with a squeak and someone quietly entered the hall.

'Who is there?' asked the doctor.

'It's me, sir . . .' said the man who had come in, in a dull voice.

The doctor's heart suddenly began to beat violently and he grew cold from shame and a kind of incomprehensible fear. The male nurse Mikhail Zakharovich (for it was he) quietly cleared his throat and entered the study with some hesitation. He waited a little and then said in a dull, guilty voice:

'I'm sorry, Grigori Ivanych!'

The doctor felt embarrassed and did not know what to say. He saw that the male nurse had come to him in order to grovel and apologise, not out of Christian humility and not for the sake of annihilating the offender with his humility, but because he had figured it all out as follows: 'I shall make an effort and will apologise, and perhaps I shan't be sacked and shan't be deprived of my daily bread. . . .' What could be more offensive to human dignity?

'I'm sorry . . .' repeated the male nurse.

'Listen . . .' began the doctor, trying not to look at him and still at a loss as to what to say. 'Listen. . . . I have offended you and . . . and I must bear the consequences, that is I must give you satisfaction. . . . You don't believe in duels. . . . As a matter of fact, I don't believe in duels either. I have offended you and you . . . you can lodge an official complaint with the J.P. and I shall pay the penalty. . . . But we cannot both of us remain here. . . . One of us, you or I, must go.' (Good heavens! I'm not saying the right thing to him! thought the doctor with horror. How silly, how silly!). 'In fact, you lodge an official complaint! But we can no longer work together! You or I. . . . Lodge it to-morrow!'

The male nurse looked sullenly at the doctor and his dark, lustreless eyes reflected the frankest possible contempt. He had always considered the doctor as an impractical and crotchety child, and now despised him for his shiver and for the incomprehensible fluster of his speech. . . .

'And so I shall,' he said with sullen spite.

'Go on then, lodge it!'

'I suppose you think I won't? I certainly shall. . . . You have no right to fight. And you ought to be ashamed of yourself. Drunken peasants may fight, but you—you're an educated man. . . .'

All the doctor's pent-up hatred suddenly flared up and he yelled at the top of his voice:

'Get out!'

The male nurse took himself off reluctantly (he gave the impression of wanting to say something else), went out into the hall and stopped there, deep in thought. Then he evidently made up his mind and resolutely left the house.

'How silly, how silly!' muttered the doctor when he had gone. 'How silly and how trite it all is!'

He felt that his behaviour towards the male nurse just then had been childish, and saw now that all his thoughts about legal proceedings were not clever, and did not solve the problem but merely complicated it.

How silly! he thought when he was sitting in his gig and afterwards when playing vint with the Military Commander.

Have I really so little education and know life so little that I'm unable to solve this simple problem? But what should I do?

The next morning the doctor saw the male nurse's wife getting into a cart and driving off somewhere and thought: She must be going to his aunt. Let her!

The hospital was carrying on without a male nurse. An official statement had to be sent to the Rural Council, and the doctor could not think of the form the letter should take. The sense of the letter was now to be as follows: 'I want you to dismiss the male nurse, though I am the guilty party, and he is not.' But to express this thought without making it sound both stupid and disgraceful was, for a decent individual, almost impossible.

Some two or three days later it was reported to the doctor that the male nurse had been to see Lev Trofimovich with an official complaint. The Chairman of the Rural Council did not let him say a single word, stamped his feet and sent him packing, screaming at him: 'I know you! Out! I don't want to listen!' From Lev Trofimovich the male nurse went to the Rural Council and there served up a libellous statement in which he did not mention the slap in the face and asked for nothing for himself but reported to the Council that the doctor had several times in his presence passed unfavourable comment on the Council and its Chairman, that the doctor gave wrong treatment, was remiss in his visits to patients, etc. When he had heard this the doctor laughed and thought: What a fool! and he felt ashamed and sorry that the male nurse should be behaving so stupidly; the more stupidly a man behaves in his own defence, the more defenceless and weak he obviously is.

Precisely a week after the morning described above the doctor received a summons from the J.P.

Now that's really silly, he thought as he signed the receipt. Nothing could be sillier.

And on his way to the J.P. one dull and quiet morning he

no longer felt ashamed, but annoyed and disgusted. He cursed himself, the male nurse and the circumstances. . . .

'I'll just say in court: go to hell all of you!' he grumbled irritably. 'You are all jackasses and you don't understand a thing!'

As he approached the J.P.'s office he saw on the threshold three of his nurses, who had been summoned as witnesses, and the mermaid. At the sight of the witnesses and the cheerful maternity nurse who was showing her impatience by shuffling from one foot to the other and who blushed from sheer delight on seeing the chief character of the forthcoming case, the doctor wanted to fly at them like a hawk and stun them with the words: 'Who has given you permission to leave the hospital? Please go back this minute,' but he forbore and tried to look calm as he made his way through the crowd of peasants to the office. The office was empty and the J.P.'s chain of office was hanging on the back of an armchair. The doctor went into the secretary's room. There he saw a thin-faced young man in a linen coat with bulging pockets—that was the secretary—and the male nurse who was sitting at a table and from nothing to do was turning over the pages of summons notices. When the doctor came in the secretary got up; the male nurse was overcome with confusion and also got up.

'Aleksandr Arkhipovich has not been in yet?' asked the doctor, feeling shy.

'Not yet. He is at home . . .' answered the secretary.

The office was situated in a lodge within the grounds of the J.P.'s park, while the J.P. himself lived in the big house. The doctor left the office and made his way slowly to the house. He found Aleksandr Arkhipovich at his samovar in the dining room. The J.P., without coat or waistcoat and with his shirt unbuttoned on the chest, was standing at the table and, holding a tea-pot with both hands, was pouring coffee-coloured tea into his glass; on seeing his guest he

quickly took another glass, filled it and asked without even
greeting him:

'Sugar or no sugar?'

A long time ago the Justice had served in the cavalry; now,
as a reward for his many years work as a J.P. he had been
given an honorary Civil Service rank, but still kept his
military uniform and his military habits. He had a long
policeman's moustache, and trousers with piping down the
side and all his words and actions were imbued with military
elegance. When he spoke he held his head slightly thrown
back, garnished his speech with juicy 'E-er's' which made
him sound like a general, shrugged his shoulders and rolled
his eyes; whenever he greeted anyone or offered a light for a
cigarette he clicked his heels, and when he walked he let his
spurs ring so carefully and tenderly as if each time they
rang it caused him unbearable pain. Having made the
doctor sit down to his tea, he patted himself on his broad
chest and belly, heaved a deep sigh and said:

'Oh yes. . . . Wouldn't you like some e-er . . . vodka
and a snack perhaps? E-er?'

'No thanks, I'm not hungry.'

Both felt that they could not avoid talking about the
hospital row, and both felt embarrassed. The doctor was
silent. The Justice with one elegant wave of his hand caught
a mosquito that had just bitten him on the chest, examined it
carefully from all sides and let it go, then sighed deeply,
looked at the doctor and asked slowly and deliberately:

'Listen, why don't you sack him?'

The doctor caught a note of sympathy in his voice; he
suddenly became sorry for himself and he felt tired and
broken as a result of the mess-up he had lived through in the
last week. He got up from the table with the air of a man
whose patience was at last exhausted, frowned in irritation
and said, shrugging his shoulders:

. 'Sack him! The way you all talk, really. . . . Amazing,
the way you all talk! How can I possibly sack him? You sit

here and think that I'm boss in my hospital and that I can do whatever I want! Amazing, the way you all talk! How can I possibly sack a male nurse if his aunt is nanny to Lev Trofimovich's children and if Lev Trofimovich needs such intriguers and flunkeys as this Zakharovich? What can I do if the local authorities don't care a brass farthing for us doctors and throw every difficulty in our path? To hell with them. I don't want to work and that's the end of it! I just don't want to!'

'Come, come now, old man. . . . You attach far too much importance, so to speak, to. . . .'

'The Marshal of Nobility tries as hard as he can to prove that we are nihilists, all of us, spies on us, and treats us as if we were his clerks. What right has he got to come to my hospital in my absence and question nurses and patients? Isn't that insulting behaviour? And that half-wit of yours, Semyon Alekseich, who walks behind his own plough and doesn't believe in medicine because he is as strong and healthy as a bull, calls us drones publicly and to our faces and grudges us a crust of bread. Damn him! I work here from morn till night, never take any rest, I'm more necessary here than all these half-wits, pious humbugs, reformers and other clowns taken together. I have sacrificed my health for the sake of my work, and all the thanks I get is to be grudged a crust of bread! Thank you very much! And everyone thinks he has the right to poke his nose into other people's business, teach, control! That Rural Councillor of yours, Kamchatski, took the doctors to task at a local government meeting because we use a lot of potassium iodide and advised us to be careful in the use of cocaine! What does he know about it, I ask you? It's none of his business! Why doesn't he teach you how to judge?'

'But then, old man, he has no manners at all, he is a boor. . . . You can't pay any attention to him.'

'No manners at all and a boor, and yet you have elected that clown to the Council and you let him poke his nose into everything! You smile, I see. You think all this is trivial and trifling, but can't you see these trifles are so numerous that life is made up of them, like a mountain out of grains of sand! I can't any more! I'm at the end of my tether, Aleksandr Arkhipych! A little more and I can assure you I'll not only slap people's faces, I'll take to shooting them! Can't you understand my nerves aren't made of steel! I'm no less of a human being than you are. . . .'

The doctor's eyes filled with tears and his voice shook; he turned away and looked out of the window. There was a silence.

'Ye-yes, my dear fellow . . .' muttered the Justice thoughtfully. 'On the other hand, if you look at it dispassionately, there is . . . (the Justice caught a mosquito, screwed up his eyes into very narrow slits, looked at it from every side, pressed it and threw it into a hand-bowl) . . . there is really no reason to sack him. Sack him and you'll get another in his place, just like him, and even perhaps a bit worse. You can change hundreds of times, but you won't find a good man . . . they're all rascals (the Justice scratched himself under the arm-pits and slowly lit a cigarette). You must reconcile yourself to this evil. I must admit tha-at nowadays you can find honest, sober and reliable workers only among the intelligentsia and the peasants, that is among these two extremes—that's all. You can, so to speak, find a very honest doctor, an excellent pedagogue, a very honest ploughman or smith, but the in-between classes, I mean, so to speak, men who have left the people but have not reached the intelligentsia, are an unreliable element. It's most difficult to find an honest and sober male nurse, clerk, bailiff and so on. Extremely difficult! Law has been my profession since the year dot and in the whole course of that time I have never had one single honest and sober clerk even though I've sacked masses of them in my day. They're people without any moral discipline, to say nothing of principles, so to speak. . . .'

What's he saying it for? thought the doctor. We are not saying the things we should.

'Well now, only last Friday,' continued the Justice, 'my Dyajinski played the following trick. Just imagine: he invited some drunkards to spend the evening with him. I'm dashed if I know who they were, and they all drank themselves silly right through the night in the office. How do you like that? I have nothing against drink. Let people drink as much as they like, but why let strangers into the office? Just think, how long would it take to filch a document or a promissory note or something out of a file? No time at all! And do you know, after that orgy I had to spend about two days checking all the files to see if anything had disappeared. . . . Well, what can you do with the rascal? Sack him? All right. . . . And where's your guarantee that the next one won't be worse?'

'Besides, how can you sack him?' said the doctor. 'It's easy enough to talk about sacking a man. . . . But how can I sack him and deprive him of a crust of bread if I know that he has a family and will go hungry? Where will he go to with his family?'

Damn it all, I'm not saying the right things! he thought and it seemed odd to him that however hard he tried he could not fix his attention on some one definite thought or some one feeling. That's because I have a shallow mind and don't know how to exercise it, he thought.

'The in-between man, as you've called him, is unreliable,' he continued. 'We sack him, curse him, slap his face, but we should really try and see things from his point of view, too. He's neither peasant nor gentry, neither fish nor fowl; his past is bitter, his present is made up of a salary of twenty-five roubles a month, a hungry family and a subordinate position, in the future he will still have the same twenty-five roubles and a subordinate position, were he to stay in his job for a hundred years. He has no education and no property; no time to read and go to church, and he can't even hear what we have to say because we don't let him come near us. And so he lives on from day to day till he dies, without a hope for a better future, on a starvation diet, terrified of being thrown out of his free flat at any moment, not knowing where his children's next home will be. And this being so, how can he possibly not take to drink or steal, you tell me that! And what principles can there be in these circumstances?'

We seem to have got on to social problems, he thought. And goodness, how incoherent we are about them, too. Good God! And what's it all for, anyway?

There was a sound of bells. Someone drove into the front yard and drove up first to the office and then to the steps of the big house.

'There he is himself,' said the Justice, looking out of the window. 'You'll get it hot and proper!'

'And you—you let me go as quickly as possible . . .' said the doctor. 'Examine my case out of turn if you can. I have no time, really.'

'All right, all right. . . . Only I don't know yet if this case comes under my jurisdiction, old man. Your relations with the male nurse are, so to speak, official, you know, and besides you biffed him in the execution of his official duties. Anyway, I don't really know. Let's ask Lev Trofimovich now.'

They heard hurried footsteps and heavy breathing and then Lev Trofimovich, the Chairman of the Rural Council, appeared in the doorway—a grey-haired old man with a bald patch, a long beard and red eye-lids.

'Good morning . . .' he said, panting. 'Ugh, My Goodness! Well, Justice, get me some *kvas!* Oh, Lord. . . .'

He lowered himself into an armchair, but jumped up at once, ran up to the doctor and staring at him angrily began to speak in a squeaky tenor:

'I'm very, I'm extremely grateful to you Grigori Ivanych! Much obliged, thank you! I'll never, never forget it!

Friends don't act this way! Think what you please, but you're really being unscrupulous even! Why didn't you let me know? Who do you think I am? Who? An enemy of yours or a stranger? Am I an enemy of yours? Have I ever refused you anything? Eh?'

Still staring and moving his fingers the Chairman drank his *kvas*, quickly wiped his lips and continued:

'Thank you very, very much, indeed! Why didn't you tell me? If you had had any feelings at all towards me, you'd have come to me and said like any friend would: "Lev Trofimovich, old man, that's how things are. . . . This is what's happened, etc., etc. . . ." I'd have fixed it for you in a trice and there would have been no need for all this scandalous business. . . . That old fool's gone right off his head, peddling his slanders all round the county, gossiping with the women, and you, disgracefully enough, if you will allow me to say so, you have started up God knows what, you've forced that fool to take legal action against you! Disgraceful, absolutely disgraceful! Everyone's asking me what the matter is, what's it all about, and here I am, the Chairman of the Rural Council, and I know nothing of what is happening at your place. You couldn't care less about me! Thank you very, very much, Grigori Ivanych!'

The Chairman made such a deep bow that he flushed crimson, then he went up to the window and shouted:

'Jigalov, tell Mikhail Zakharych to come here! Tell him to come this minute! You ought to be ashamed of yourself!' he said, as he left the window. 'Even my wife felt hurt, and yet you couldn't be more of a favourite of hers. The trouble with you people is that you are all trying to be too clever! You're all eager to do things in oh! such a clever way and all according to principles and all with such cunning embellishments and all you succeed in doing is simply to cast aspersions on others.'

'You are eager not to be too clever, and what do you succeed in doing?' asked the doctor.

'What do we succeed in doing? What we succeed in doing is that if I hadn't arrived here you would have disgraced both yourself and us. . . . You should count yourself lucky that I have arrived!'

The male nurse came in and halted on the threshold. The Chairman stood sideways to him, put his hands in his pockets, cleared his throat and said:

'Apologise to the doctor at once!'

The doctor blushed and rushed out of the room.

'There, you see, the doctor doesn't want to accept your apologies!' continued the Chairman. 'He wants you to prove that you are really sorry by the way you behave and not merely in words. Do you give me your word that from this day onwards you will obey and will lead a sober existence?'

'I do . . .' said the male nurse sullenly in a deep bass.

'Look out now! You better be careful! You'll lose your job in no time if I have anything to do with it! If anything happens, don't go about begging for mercy. . . . Well, go home now. . . .'

To the male nurse, who had by then become reconciled to his misfortune, such a turn of events was an unexpected surprise. He even turned pale from sheer joy. He wanted to say something and stretched out his hand, but said nothing, smiled sheepishly and went out.

'That's that!' said the Chairman. 'And no need for a court case.'

He heaved a sigh of relief and with an air of having just accomplished something very difficult and important examined the samovar and the glasses, rubbed his hands and said:

'Blessed are the peacemakers. . . . Do pour me out a glass, Aleksandr. But perhaps you could let us have something to eat first. . . . A drop of vodka, too, perhaps. . . .'

'Look here, it's impossible!' said the doctor coming back into the dining room, still red in the face, and wringing his hands. 'It's—it's a comedy! It's wicked! I can't. I'd sooner have a hundred court cases than solve problems so farcically. No, I can't!'

'What do you want, then?' snapped back the chairman. 'Sack him? All right, I shall. . . .'

'No, not sack him. I don't know what I want . . . but to have such an attitude to life. . . . Oh, goodness me! It's torture!'

The doctor began to fuss about nervously and look for his hat, did not find it and sank exhausted into an armchair.

'Wicked!' he repeated.

'My dear fellow,' whispered the Justice. 'I don't quite understand you, so to speak. . . . After all, you are the guilty party in this incident! Slapping people's faces at the end of the nineteenth century—in a way, you know, this is not quite the thing. . . . He is a rascal, bu-u-t you must agree you behaved rashly, too. . . .'

'Of course!' agreed the Chairman.

Vodka and snacks were brought in. Before saying goodbye the doctor ate a radish and washed it down with one glass of vodka. He did it quite mechanically. On his way back to the hospital, his thoughts were gradually being covered over with mist like grass on an autumn morning.

Can it really be, he thought, that in the course of this last week people have suffered, thought and said so much for everything only to end in this trite and incongruous way! How silly! How silly!

He was ashamed of having implicated strangers in his personal problem, ashamed of the words he had said to these strangers, of the vodka he had drunk out of habit, to drink and live to no set purpose, ashamed of his shallow and un-understanding mind. As soon as he was back in hospital he immediately began his round of the wards. The male nurse walked beside him, stepping softly like a cat, and softly answering questions. . . . The male nurse and the mermaid and the other nurses pretended that nothing had happened and that everything was all right. And the doctor, too, did everything in his power to appear indifferent. He gave orders, lost his temper, joked with the patients, but one thought buzzed in his mind:

Silly, silly, silly. . . .

THE EVE OF THE TRIAL

The Defendant's Story

❋

'SURE to be trouble, sir!' said the coachman, turning towards me, and pointing with his whip at a hare running across our road.

I had no need of a hare to tell me that my future was desperate. I was driving to the district assizes at X——, where I had to appear in the dock for bigamy. The weather was terrible. When, towards nightfall, I arrived at the post-station, I was so chilled, soaked and stupefied by the monotonous jolting of the road that I looked like a man who had been covered with snow, drenched with water, and badly whacked. I was met at the station by the station-super-intendent, a tall man in blue-striped underpants, bald, sleepy, and with a moustache which seemed to grow out of his nostrils and looked as if it would prevent him from smelling anything.

And it must be admitted that there was plenty to smell. When the supervisor, muttering something, breathing heavily through his nose and scratching his neck, opened the door of the station 'rest-room' and silently showed me my place of rest with his elbow, I was overwhelmed—almost to suffocation—by a strong smell of something sour, sealing-wax, and squashed bugs. The unpainted wooden walls were illuminated by a small tin lamp which stood on the table and was smoking like matchwood.

'Your place certainly stinks, signor!' I said, going in and putting my suitcase on the table.

The supervisor sniffed the air and shook his head incredulously.

'Smells as it always does,' he said, and scratched himself. 'That's just your impression, coming from outside. The coachmen sleep with their horses, and the gentlemen don't smell.'

I dismissed the supervisor, and began inspecting my temporary abode. The sofa on which I would have to recline was as wide as a double bed, covered with oilcloth, and as cold as ice. Apart from the sofa, the room contained a large iron stove, the table with the above-mentioned lamp, someone's felt boots, someone's travelling hand-bag, and a screen which barricaded one corner of the room. Behind the screen someone was peacefully sleeping. When I had made my inspection I made the sofa ready for the night and began to undress. My nose soon became accustomed to the stench. I took off my frock-coat, trousers and boots, stretched and scratched to my heart's content, smiled, hugged myself and began to skip round the iron stove, raising high my bare feet. . . . This skipping warmed me up even more. After that it only remained to lie down on the sofa and go to sleep, but at that moment something odd happened. By chance my glance fell on the screen and . . . imagine my horror! A woman's head, with loose hair, black eyes, and teeth bared, was looking at me from behind the screen. Her black eyebrows were twitching, pretty little dimples were playing on her cheeks—so she must have been laughing. I was embarrassed. The head, noticing that I had seen it, also became embarrassed, and hid. With eyes cast down and a guilty look, I went meekly to the sofa, lay down, and covered myself with my fur coat.

What a business! I thought. That means she saw me skipping! That's too bad. . . .

And, as I recalled the features of that pretty little face, I fell to dreaming. Pictures, each more beautiful and seductive than the last, thronged in my imagination and . . . and, as if to punish me for sinful thoughts, a sharp pain suddenly burned my right cheek. I clutched at it, caught nothing, but guessed what had happened: there was a smell of squashed bug.

At the same moment I heard a woman's voice. 'It really is the very devil! These damned bugs obviously want to eat me up!'

Mm! . . . I remembered my good habit of always taking insect powder with me when I travelled. And I had not changed my habit this time. I took the tin of powder out of my suitcase in a matter of seconds. It only remained to offer the pretty head a remedy for bugs and—friendship would be struck up. But how could I offer it?

'This is awful!'

'Madam,' I said in my most honeyed tones. 'If I understand your last exclamation rightly, you are being bitten by bugs. Now, I have some insect powder. If you wish, then. . . .'

'Oh yes, please!'

'In that case,' I said, delighted, 'I'll just . . . put on my fur coat and bring it to you. . . .'

'No, no . . . give it me through the screen, but don't come here!'

'Of course I meant through the screen. Don't be afraid: I'm not a bashi-bazouk. . . .'

'Who knows? You're just a passer-by, after all. . . .'

'Mm. . . . And even if I was to go behind the screen . . . there wouldn't be much harm in it . . . all the more so as I'm a doctor,' I lied. 'Doctors, policemen, and ladies' hair-dressers have the right to intrude in people's private lives.'

'Is it true that you're a doctor? Seriously?'

'Word of honour. So may I bring you the insect powder?'

'Well, if you're a doctor, I suppose. . . . But why should you have the trouble? I can send my husband to you. . . . Fedya!' said the brunette, dropping her voice. 'Fedya! Wake up, you mutt! Get up and go round the screen! The doctor's so kind, he's offering us some insect powder.'

The presence of 'Fedya' behind the screen was shattering

news to me. I was thunderstruck. . . . My heart was filled with the feeling which, in all probability, rifle-cocks feel after a miss-fire: shame, vexation, and sorrow. . . . I felt so upset about it and, when he appeared from behind the screen, I felt that Fedya must be such a scoundrel that I almost shouted for help. Fedya turned out to be a tall, sinewy man of about fifty, with little grey whiskers, the set lips of a civil servant, and with blue veins running untidily over his nose and temples. He was in dressing-gown and slippers.

'It's very kind of you, doctor . . .' he said, taking the insect powder from me and turning round to go back behind the screen. 'Merci. . . . You were caught by the snow-storm too?'

'Yes!' I snarled, lying down on the sofa and furiously pulling the fur coat over me. 'Yes!'

'I see. . . . Zinochka, there's a bug running down your little nose! Allow me to remove it!'

'All right!' laughed Zinochka. 'You didn't get it! You're a senior civil servant, everyone's afraid of you, but you can't deal with a bug!'

'Zinochka, in front of strangers . . . (a sigh). You're always. . . . Honestly. . . .'

'The swine! They won't let me sleep!' I grumbled, getting angry without myself knowing why.

But soon husband and wife fell silent. I closed my eyes and, in order to fall asleep, began to think of nothing at all. But half an hour, an hour passed . . . and I was not asleep. Finally my neighbours, too, began to toss and turn and grumble in whispers.

'It's amazing, even insect powder doesn't do any good!' growled Fedya. 'There's so many of them, these bugs! Doctor! Zinochka wants me to ask you why these bugs smell so loathesomely?'

We chatted. We talked about bugs, the weather, the Russian winter, medicine—which I know about as much

about as I do about astronomy—we talked about
Edison. . . .

'Don't be shy, Zinochka. . . . After all, he's a doctor!'
I heard a whisper after the conversation about Edison. 'Don't
stand on ceremony, ask him. . . . There's nothing to be
afraid of. Shervetsov didn't do any good, perhaps this one
will. . . .'

'Ask yourself!' whispered Zinochka.

'Doctor,' said Fedya, addressing himself to me. 'Why
does my wife get a congestion in her chest sometimes? A
cough, you know . . . it feels congested, you know, a sort
of clot. . . .'

'That's a long story, it's impossible to say at once . . .' I
replied, trying to dodge the question.

'Well, what if it is a long story? We've got plenty of time
. . . we aren't sleeping anyway. . . . Have a look at her,
old fellow! I should tell you, Shervetsov is treating her. . . .
He's a good man, but . . . who can tell? I've no faith in
him! No faith at all! I can see you don't want to, but do be
so kind! You examine her, and while you're doing it I'll
go to the superintendent and order a samovar to be put on.'

Fedya shuffled off in his slippers and left the room. I
went behind the screen. Zinochka was sitting on a wide sofa,
surrounded by a quantity of pillows, and holding up her lace
collar.

'Show me your tongue!' I began, sitting down beside her
and frowning.

She put out her tongue and laughed. It was an ordinary,
red tongue. I tried to feel her pulse.

'Mm! . . .' I mooed, unable to find the pulse.

I cannot remember what other questions I put to her as
I looked at her little laughing face—I only remember that
by the time I had finished examining her I felt such a silly
idiot that I definitely could not cope with any more
questions.

It all ended with Fedya, Zinochka and myself sitting

round the samovar; a prescription had to be written, and I composed it according to all the rules of medicine:

Rp. Sic transit   0.05
Gloria Mundi   1.0
Aquae destillatae   0.1
One table-spoonful every two hours.
    Mrs. Syelov.
                Dr. Zaitsev.

In the morning I was on the point of leaving and, with suitcase in hand, was saying farewell for ever to my new friends, when Fedya buttonholed me and, holding a ten rouble note, tried to make me take it:

'Oh, but it's your duty to take it! I always pay for all honest labour! You've studied and you've worked! You've sweated blood to acquire your knowledge! I understand that!'

There was nothing else to be done, I had to take the ten roubles!

That, in general outline, is how I spent the eve of my trial. I will not describe my feelings when the door opened in front of me and the bailiff showed me into the dock. I will only say that I grew pale and embarrassed when, looking round, I saw thousands of eyes fixed on me; and I felt my last hour had come when I looked at the serious, solemnly important faces of the jury. . . .

But I cannot describe—and you cannot imagine—my horror when, raising my eyes to the table covered with red cloth, I saw in the public prosecutor's place—whom do you think?—Fedya! He was sitting there and writing something. As I looked at him I remembered the bugs, Zinochka, my examination of her—and it was not a mere shiver that ran down my spine, but the whole Arctic ocean. . . . When he had finished writing, he looked at me. At first he did not recognise me, but then his pupils dilated and his jaw dropped weakly . . . his hands shook. He got up slowly and fixed a glassy stare on me. I too got up, not knowing myself why I did so, and stared at him. . . .

'Will the defendant please tell the court his name and particulars?' the judge began.

The public prosecutor sat down and drank a glass of water. Cold sweat broke out on his forehead.

Well, now I'm for it! I thought.

Everything pointed to the fact that the Public Prosecutor was determined to cook my goose. He kept on losing his temper, went minutely into the witnesses' evidence, was crotchety, grumbled. . . .

However, it's time I finished this. I am writing it in the court-room during the luncheon interval. . . . In a moment the Prosecutor will make his speech.

I wonder what will happen?

SINISTER NIGHT

(*A Sketch*)

❊

Dogs are barking—a short, snappy bark, followed by a
nervous howl—like that of dogs that scent an enemy, but
are unable to understand who or where it is. A variety of
sounds float in the autumn air, disturbing the silence of the
night: an indistinct murmur of human voices, a fussy, uneasy
bustle, the squeak of a gate, the stamping of a horse.

Three dark figures are standing on an empty flower-bed in
the courtyard of Dyadin's farm, in front of the terrace of the
manor house. Semyon, the night-watchman, is easily
recognisable by his bell-shaped sheep-skin coat tied round
with a string and with tufts of wool hanging down from it.
Next to him stands a tall, spindly-legged man with sticking-
out ears, dressed in a jacket—that is Gavrila, the footman.
The third, wearing a waistcoat and shirt hanging outside his
trousers, a rough-hewn man resembling one of those wooden
toy men, is the coachman, and is also called Gavrila. All
three are holding on to a wooden palisade and looking into
the distance.

'Holy Virgin, have mercy on us,' murmurs Semyon in a
voice charged with emotion. 'Terrible it is, terrible! The
wrath of the Lord is upon us. . . . Holy Virgin. . . .'

'It's not far away, boys . . .' says Gavrila the footman in
a bass voice. 'About four miles, no more. . . . I should say
it's at the German farms. . . .'

He is interrupted by Gavrila the coachman: 'The German
farms are more to the left. They are over there, the German
farms, if you look at that there birch-tree. . . . At Kreshchenskoye, it is.'

'It's at Kreshchenskoye,' Semyon agrees.

Someone runs barefoot across the terrace, his heels striking the ground with a dull thud, and slams a door. The manor house is plunged in sleep. The pitch-black windows have a sullen, autumnal look about them, and only one of them shows a dim, weak light thrown by a small lamp protected by a pink shade. The young mistress, Maria Sergeyevna, is sleeping in the room with the lamp. Her husband, Nikolai Alexeyevich, has gone somewhere to play cards, and has not yet returned.

'Nastasya!' someone shouts.

'The mistress is awake,' says Gavrila the footman. 'Wait a bit, you two, I'll go and tell her what to do. She must let me take the horses and men, as many as there are, and I'll drive over to Kreshchenskoye and deal with that there in no time at all. . . . Dull-witted people they are over there. Blockheads. I'll give them instructions what to do.'

'You'll give them instructions all right! Look at him— wants to give people instructions and can't keep his own teeth from chattering! There are plenty of people there without you. . . . Police officers and constables and gentry —they are all there, I dare say.'

A glass door leading on to the terrace gives a clanking noise as it opens, and the mistress of the house makes her appearance.

'What's happening? What's all this noise?' she asks, coming up to the three silhouettes. 'Is that you, Semyon?'

Before Semyon has time to answer, she recoils in horror and throws up her hands.

'My God, what a disaster!' she exclaims. 'Has it been going on for long? Where is it? And why didn't you wake me?'

The whole southern half of the sky has flushed crimson. The sky looks inflamed and tense, and the sinister glow twinkles and shivers as if pulsating. Clouds, hillocks and bare trees stand out in high relief against the enormous crimson background. The hurried, fitful sounds of the tocsin can be heard.

'It's terrible, terrible,' says the mistress. 'Where's the fire?'

'Not far away, in Kreshchenskoye. . . .'

'Oh, my God! Nikolai Alexeyevich is not at home, and I don't know what to do. Does the bailiff know?'

'He does, madam. . . . He's gone over there with three barrels.'

'Poor people!'

'And the worst of it is, madam, there's no river there. There's a rotten little pond, but even that's not in the village itself.'

'As if water could put it out!' says Gavrila the footman. 'The main thing is not to let the fire spread. They need people with some understanding who'd make them demolish cottages. . . . May I have your permission to go there, madam?'

'There's no need for you to go,' replies Maria Sergeyevna. 'You'll only be in the way.'

Gavrila coughs to indicate that he has taken offence, and walks away. Semyon and the other Gavrila, who cannot stand the cleverness and the haughty tone of the footman in the jacket, are very pleased with the mistress's rebuke.

'Of course he'd only be in the way!' says Semyon.

And both of them, night-watchman and coachman, as if eager to show off the gravity of their outlook in front of their mistress, begin to pour out holy sentiments:

'The Lord has punished them for their sins. . . . That's what it is! Man sins and takes no thought of it, but the Lord is there to sort of. . . .'

The sight of the crimson sky affects them all in the same way. Mistress and servants alike suffer from an internal shiver and feel cold, so cold that they cannot keep their hands, heads and voices from shaking. . . . They may be afraid, but they are even more impatient. . . . They want to climb higher up, to see the actual fire, the smoke, the people. A thirst for strong sensations gets the better of fear and sympathy for other people's grief. Whenever the glow grows paler or seems to diminish, Gavrila the coachman, declares joyfully:

'Well, it looks as if they're putting it out! May the Lord help them!'

But nevertheless a note of regret can be heard in his voice. And whenever the glow flares up and seems to expand, he sighs and throws up his hands in despair, but to judge by the panting and the puffing which accompany his efforts to stand up on tiptoes he must feel a certain pleasure. They all realise that they are witnessing a horrible disaster and they all shiver; but were the fire suddenly to stop they would have a feeling of dissatisfaction. Such a contradictory attitude is natural, and man—a selfish creature—should not be reproached with it. Beauty, however sinister, is beauty none the less, and human sentiment cannot refrain from paying tribute to it.

A faint sound of thunder can be heard: someone is treading heavily on the iron roof of the house.

'Is that you, Vanka?' shouts Semyon.

'It's me and Nastasya!'

'You'll fall, damn you! See anything?'

'Ye-es! It's at Kreshchenskoye, boys!'

'One could probably see from the dormer window,' said Maria Sergeyevna. 'Shall we go and look from there?'

The sight of disaster draws people together. The mistress, forgetting her pride, Semyon and the two Gavrilas enter the house. Pale, trembling from fear and craving for sensation, they go through all the rooms and climb the stairs to the attic. It is dark everywhere, and the candle held by Gavrila the footman does not make it any lighter, but only throws dim patches of light around. The mistress sees the attic for the first time in her life. . . . The beams, dark corners, stove pipes, the smell of dust and spider webs, the strange, earthy ground under her feet—all this gives her an impression of a décor for a fairy-tale.

So that's where the hobgoblins live? she thinks.

From the dormer window the glow appears wider and more crimson. The fire itself can be seen. A long, bright-gold band stretches across the horizon. It moves and plays like quick-silver.

'It's certainly not just one cottage that's burning. Half the village's caught, I should say,' says Gavrila the coachman.

'Listen! The bell's stopped ringing—the church must be on fire now.'

'And it's a wooden church, too!' says the mistress, choking from the heavy smell given out by Semyon's sheepskin coat. 'What a catastrophe!'

When they have had a good look they go downstairs. Soon afterwards the master, Nikolai Alexeyevich, arrives. He has had a good deal to drink with his friends, and now, curled up in his carriage like a kitten, he snores loudly. They wake him up. He looks stupidly at the glow and mutters:

'A hor . . . horse! Qu . . . quick!'

'Don't!' protests Maria Sergeyevna. 'How can you possibly go anywhere in the condition you're in? Go to bed!'

'A hor . . . horse!' he orders, swaying.

A horse is brought. He climbs into the saddle, shakes his head, and disappears in the darkness. Meanwhile the dogs howl and strain, as if smelling a wolf. Women and boys collect around Semyon and the two Gavrilas. There is no end to the moans and the groans and the sighs and the signs of the cross they make. A man on horseback gallops into the yard.

'Six people burnt to death,' he mumbles, panting. 'Half the village—gone! Cattle lost too—goodness knows how many. The carpenter's—Stepan's—old woman—burnt to death.'

The mistress's impatience reaches its bursting point. The

movement and the talk egg her on. She orders the carriage and drives over to the fire herself. The night is dark and cold. The light, pre-dawn frost has slightly hardened the ground, and the horses' hooves make a dull thud on it, as if on a carpet. Gavrila the footman is sitting on the box beside the coachman and fidgets impatiently. He looks around, mutters to himself, continually gets up with an air which gives the impression that the fate of Kreshchenskoye depends on him. . . .

'The main thing is not to let the fire spread . . .' he mumbles. 'You must know how, whatever you do, and what do those country yokels know?'

After driving about three or four miles the mistress sees something so extraordinary, so monstrous, that few people ever see it, and then only once in a lifetime, something not even the richest imagination could invent. The village is burning like an enormous bonfire. The entire field of vision is obscured by a sheet of moving, blinding flame, into which cottages, trees and church sink as into fog. Light almost as bright as sunlight blends with volumes of black smoke and lustreless steam, golden tongues slither up and down and lick the blackened shells of buildings with a greedy crackle, smiling and gaily winking as they do it. Clouds of red, golden dust drift swiftly to the sky and, as if to complete the picture, startled doves plunge into them. The air is filled with a strange medley of sounds: a monstrous crackle, the flapping of flames, resembling the flapping of thousands of birds' wings, human voices, bleating, mooing, the squeak of wheels. The church is awe-inspiring. Flames and clouds of thick smoke pour out of its windows. The steeple hangs down like a black giant in a mass of light and golden dust; it is completely charred, but the bells still hang, and it is difficult to see what is holding them. . . .

There is a jostling crowd on either side of the road, reminiscent of a fair or the first ferry-boat after the spring tides. People, horses, loaded carts, barrels, piles of personal possessions. All this moves, mixes, makes noises. The mistress contemplates this chaos, and hears her husband's shrill cry:

'Send him to the hospital! Pour water over him!'

Gavrila the footman stands on top of a loaded cart and waves his arms. Lit up by the fire he cast a long shadow, and he seems taller. . . .

'Arson—that sticks out a mile,' he shouts, whirling round like one possessed. 'Hey, you there! You shouldn't let the fire spread! You mustn't let it spread!'

All around one sees pale, dull, seemingly wooden faces. Dogs howl, hens cluck. . . .

'Look out!' cry the coachmen of neighbouring landowners who have driven over.

It is an extraordinary picture! Maria Sergeyevna cannot believe her eyes, and only the intense heat makes her realise that it is not a dream. . . .

THE LODGER

✦

BRYKOVICH, a young, but prematurely bald, man rushed out of his flat onto the landing one midnight and slammed the door with all his might. He had formerly been a working lawyer, but was now doing nothing and living at the expense of his rich wife, the owner of an establishment called 'Tunis' containing furnished rooms to let.

'Oh, the wicked, stupid, dull witch!' he muttered, clenching his fists. 'Why has the Devil tied me to you! . . . Ugh! . . . I'd need to be a cannon to shout louder than that hell-cat!'

Brykovich was choking with fury and indignation, and if at that moment, as he was pacing the long corridor of the 'Tunis', he had come across some household utensil or a sleepy floor-waiter, he would have been only too delighted to give free play to his hands so as to work off his anger on something. He wanted to swear, scream, stamp his feet. . . . And fate, as if it understood his mood and wanted to gain his favour, brought him face to face with Khalyavkin, a musician who lived in Room No. 31 and was always late with his rent. Khalyavkin was standing in front of his own door, prodding the keyhole with his key and swaying visibly as he did so. He was breathing noisily and was sending someone to hell; but the key would not obey him and hit the wrong target every time. He was prodding convulsively with one hand and holding a violin case in the other. Brykovich swooped down on him like a hawk and shouted angrily: 'Ah, it's you? Look here, my good man, when are you going to pay the rent? You haven't paid for a whole fortnight, my good man! I'll tell them not to heat your stove. I'll have you evicted, my dear sir. Damn you!'

'You are in my w . . . way . . .' answered the musician calmly. 'Ore . . . rewar!'

'You ought to be ashamed of yourself, Mr. Khalyavkin!' continued Brykovich. 'You get one hundred and twenty roubles a month and could be punctual in your payments! It's unconscientious, my dear sir! It's mean to a degree.'

At last the key clicked and the door opened.

'I mean, it's dishonest!' continued Brykovich following the musician into the room. 'I warn you, if you don't pay to-morrow, not later than to-morrow I'll take legal action. I'll show you! And please be good enough not to throw lighted matches on the floor; you might set fire to my house! I will not have people of inebriate habits living in my rooms.'

Khalyavkin looked at Brykovich with his drunken, laughing eyes and grinned.

'I really don't see why you are getting so worked up . . .' he muttered, lighting a cigarette and burning his fingers. 'I don't see it! I don't pay my rent, agreed; I know I don't pay, but what's that got to do with you, can you tell me? What do you care? You don't pay any rent either, but I never pester you about it. You don't pay—all right then, don't.'

'But how do you mean?'

'Just so . . . the la . . . landlord here is not you, but your most respected spouse. . . . Here you . . . here you are just as much of a damned lodger as any one else. . . . The rooms aren't yours, so what are you worrying about? You take my example: I don't worry, do I? You don't pay a farthing's rent—and so what? Don't—if you don't want to. I am not worrying.'

'I don't understand you, my dear sir!' muttered Brykovich and assumed the pose of a man who has been insulted and is ready at any moment to defend his honour.

'My fault, though! I quite forgot that you acquired the rooms as your wife's dowry. . . . My fault! Though, as a matter of fact, if you look at it from the moral point of view,' continued Khalyavkin, still swaying, 'you mustn't get worked up, all the same. . . . After all, you acquired them for no . . . nothing, for a pinch of snuff. . . . They are, if you look at it broadly, just as much yours as mine. . . . How did you app . . . appropriate them? By becoming the husband? . . . That's not much to boast of! It isn't a bit difficult to be a husband. You bring me twelve dozen wives here, my dear sir, and I'll be husband to all of them—free of charge! Do me the favour!'

The musician's drunken chatter apparently touched Brykovich on his sorest spot. He blushed and for a long time did not know what to answer, then came up to Khalyavkin and giving him a furious look, struck the table with his fist with all his might.

'How dare you say this to me?' he hissed. 'How dare you?'

'Now, now,' muttered Khalyavkin, backing away. 'That's playing it fortissimo. I don't see why you should take offence. I . . . I mean no offence, I mean it . . . as a compliment. If I were ever to come across a lady with such damn fine rooms, I'd snatch her up lock, stock and barrel . . . you just show her to me!'

'But . . . but how dare you insult me?' shouted Brykovich, and again struck the table with his fist.

'I don't understand!' said Khalyavkin, shrugging his shoulders and no longer smiling. 'But as a matter of fact, I'm drunk . . . perhaps I have insulted you. . . . In that case, I'm sorry, my fault! My dear fellow, forgive the first violin! I didn't want to cause offence in the very slightest.'

'It's cynical even . . .' said Brykovich mollified by Khalyavkin's repentant tone of voice. 'There are things people don't talk about in that way. . . .'

'All right, all right. . . .I won't! My dear fellow, I won't! Your hand!'

'Particularly, as I gave no occasion to . . .' continued Brykovich, in a hurt voice, completely mollified, and now stretching out his hand. 'I never did you any harm.'

8

'True enough, I shouldn't have ra . . . raised this ticklish problem. . . . I let it slip off my tongue, like a fool, in my cups. . . . Sorry, old man! I really am a brute! I'll now pour cold water on my head and get sober.'

'It's a foul life, as it is, loathesome, and you add to it all with your insults!' Brykovich was saying, as he paced the room in his excitement. 'No-one sees the truth and everyone thinks and babbles as he likes. I can imagine what is being said behind one's back in these rooms! I can just imagine it! True I was wrong, it was my fault: it was silly of me to attack you in the middle of the night because of money; my fault, but . . . after all, you must excuse me, enter into my position, and yet . . . you throw filthy hints into my face!'

'My dear fellow, I'm drunk, don't you see! I repent and feel for you. Honest to God I do. And I'll let you have the money, old boy! As soon as I get it on the first of the month, I'll let you have it! Peace and harmony, then! Hurrah! Oh, my dear fellow, I love educated people! I studied myself once, in the Musical Acadecademy . . . can't say it right, damn! . . .'

Tears welled up in Khalyavkin's eyes, he caught Brykovich by the sleeve as the latter was pacing up and down, and kissed him on the cheek. . . . 'Ah, my dear friend, I'm as drunk as a coot, but I can see it all. Tell the floor-waiter to bring the first violin a samovar, old boy! You have a strict rule here—No walking about the corridor and no ordering of samovars after eleven o'clock; but it's something terrible how thirsty one is after the theatre!'

Brykovich pressed the bell-button. 'Timofey, bring a samovar for Mr. Khalyavkin!' he said to the floor-waiter who had now appeared.

'Can't be done, sir!' boomed out Timofey in a deep bass. 'Madame has told us not to serve up samovars after eleven o'clock.'

'Well then, I order you to!' shouted Brykovich turning pale.

'No use ordering, if we are told not to . . .' grumbled the floor-waiter, leaving the room. 'Can't be done if we are told not to. And that's that!'

Brykovich bit his lip, turned his head away and looked out of the window.

'What a position to be in!' sighed Khalyavkin. 'Er, yes, I must say. . . . Oh well, no use my feeling embarrassed, I understand, you know . . . your innermost self. All that psychology, I know it all. . . . Well then, there's nothing to be done, you have to drink vodka, willy-nilly, if they don't give you tea! Will you have some vodka, eh?'

Khalyavkin got a bottle of vodka and a sausage from the window-sill and made himself comfortable on the sofa to start on his drink and his snacks. Brykovich sadly contemplated the sot and listened to his endless prattle. Perhaps because at the sight of that tousled head, the half-pint bottle and the cheap sausage, he remembered his recent past, when he was just as poor, but free, and the expression on his face became yet gloomier, and he felt he wanted a drink. He came up to the table, emptied a glass and coughed.

'It's a horrid life!' he said and shook his head. 'Foul! You see—you've just insulted me, the floor-waiter has insulted me . . . and so it goes on! . . . And why? Just like that, for no reason really. . . .'

After his third, Brykovich sat down on the sofa and became thoughtful, propping up his head in his hands, then he sighed sadly and said:

'I made a big mistake! Oh, what a mistake! I've sold my youth and career and principles—that's why life is taking its revenge on me now. A desperate revenge.'

The vodka and the sad thoughts made him very pale and even seemed to have made him thinner, several times he clutched his head in despair and said: 'Oh, what a life, if you only knew!'

'Admit now, tell me honestly,' he said, peering into Khalyavkin's face, 'Tell me in all conscience, what do people

here in general . . . think of me? What do the students
living in these rooms say? I'm sure you've heard. . . .'

'I have. . . .'

'Well, what?'

'They don't say anything, they just despise you.'

The new friends talked no more. They did not separate
till dawn, when the servants began lighting stoves in the
corridor.

'Don't you pay her . . . anything . . .' Brykovich was
muttering as he left. 'Don't pay her a penny! Let it be. . . .'

Khalyavkin fell on the sofa, put his head on the violin case
and snored loudly.

The following midnight they met again. . . .

Having partaken of the joys of friendly libations Brykovich
never misses a single night now, and if he finds Khalyavkin
is out, he goes into someone else's room, where he bemoans
his fate and drinks, drinks and bemoans it again—and this
he does every night.

THE DREAM

A Christmas Story

SOMETIMES the weather in winter, as if vexed by human infirmity, enlists grim autumn's help and works in co-operation with it. Snow and rain whirl about in the gloomy, foggy air. The wind—raw, cold and piercing—knocks at the windows and roofs with violent fury. It howls in the chimneys and weeps in the ventilators. Dejection hangs in the air, which is black as soot. . . . Nature feels sick. . . . Everything is raw, cold and uncanny. . . .

It was just that sort of weather on Christmas Eve, 1882, before I became a convict, when I was working as a valuer in the pawnshop of Tupayev, a retired captain.

It was midnight. The store-room—in which, at the boss's wish, I had my night abode and acted as a watch-dog—was weakly lit by the blue flame of a small wick floating in oil. It was a large, square room, cluttered up with bundles, trunks, what-nots. . . . On the grey wooden walls—from the chinks of which peeped out bits of tow—hung hare-skin and cloth coats, guns, pictures, a sconce, a guitar. . . . As it was my duty to guard all this property at night I lay behind the showcase on a big red trunk full of valuables, and looked thoughtfully at the flame of the lamp.

For some reason, I felt frightened. Things kept in the store-room of a pawnshop are frightening. . . . At night time, in the dim light of the lamp, they seem alive. . . . And that evening, while the rain muttered outside the window, and the wind howled mournfully in the stove and above the ceiling, it seemed to me as if they too were howling.

99

Before they had turned up here they had all had to pass through the valuer's hands—that is, through mine—so I knew everything about every one of them. . . . I knew, for instance, that powders for a consumptive cough had been bought with the money obtained for that guitar. . . . I knew that a dunkard had shot himself with that revolver; his wife had hidden the revolver from the police, pawned it at our shop, and bought a coffin. A bracelet which was looking at me from the showcase had been pawned by the man who had stolen it. . . . Two lace chemises, marked No. 178, had been pawned by a girl who needed a rouble to get into a *Salon* where she intended to earn some money. . . . In a word, on each article I read hopeless sorrow, illness, crime, venal debauch. . . .

On Christmas Eve these things were somehow particularly eloquent.

'Let us go home! . . .' it seemed to me that they were weeping with the wind. 'Let us go!'

But it was not only the things that provoked a feeling of terror in me. Whenever I raised my head above the showcase and threw a timid glance at the dark, misted window, it seemed to me that human faces were looking into the store-room from the street.

'What nonsense!' I nerved myself. 'What silly sentimentality.'

The fact was that a man endowed by nature with the nerves of a valuer was, on Christmas Eve, tormented by his conscience—an incredible and almost fantastic occurrence. The only conscience allowed in pawnshops is a pawned conscience; there it is understood to be an article that can be bought and sold—no other functions for it are recognised. Where on earth could I have got it from? I tossed from side to side on my hard trunk and, screwing up my eyes against the flickering lamp, I tried with all my strength to smother this new and unbidden feeling within me. But my efforts remained vain. . . .

Of course, physical and mental exhaustion after a heavy day's work was partly to blame. On Christmas Eve the poor used to press into the pawnshop in crowds. On an important feast-day, and in foul weather into the bargain, poverty is no crime, but a terrible misfortune! At such a time the poor look for a crumb in the pawnshop and receive a stone in its stead. . . . On Christmas Eve so many people came to see us that we had to take three-quarters of the pawned goods into the barn because we had no room in the store-room. From early morning till late at night, without stopping for a moment, I had haggled with paupers, squeezed pennies and half-pennies out of them, seen their tears, listened to their vain entreaties. . . . By the end of the day I could hardly stand on my feet: I was tired out, body and soul. It was not surprising that I could not sleep now, that I was tossing from side to side and feeling frightened. . . .

Someone knocked cautiously on my door. . . . After the knock I heard the boss's voice:

'Are you asleep, Pyotr Demyanich?'

'No, not yet. Why?'

'You know, I've been thinking, shouldn't we open the doors early to-morrow morning? It's Christmas Day, and the weather's awful. The poor will rush to us, like flies to honey. So you'd better not go to Mass to-morrow, but sit at the till. . . . Good night!'

'I feel frightened,' I decided when the boss had left, 'because the lamp is flickering. . . . I must put it out. . . .'

I got out of bed and went to the corner where the lamp was hanging. The little blue flame spluttered weakly and flickered, and was clearly in the throes of death. Each flicker lit up the ikon, the walls, the bundles, the dark window for an instant. . . . And through the window two pale faces, pressed against the glass, were looking into the store-room.

'There's no one there . . .' I argued. 'I'm imagining it.'

When, after blowing out the light, I was groping my way

to the bed, something odd happened which had a considerable influence on my subsequent mood. A loud, shrill twang suddenly and unexpectedly resounded above my head, but lasted no more than a second. Something cracked and gave a loud whine, as if in great pain.

A string had broken on the guitar, but I was seized by panic fear and, stuffing up my ears, ran like a madman to the bed, tripping over the trunks and bundles. . . . I buried my head in the pillow and listened, hardly daring to breathe, my heart in my mouth.

'Let us go!' howled the wind and the things together. 'Let us go, for Christmas's sake! After all, you're a pauper too, you understand! You too have been through hunger and cold! Let us go!'

Yes, I had been a pauper too, and I knew what hunger and cold were like. Poverty had pushed me into the damned job of being a valuer, poverty had forced me to despise grief and tears for the sake of a crust of bread. If it had not been for poverty, would I have had sufficient courage to value in pence what is worth health, warmth, holiday joys? Of what, then, was the wind accusing me? Why was my conscience tormenting me?

But no matter how hard my heart was beating, no matter how fear and a gnawing conscience tormented me, exhaustion won the day. I fell asleep. I slept lightly. . . . I heard the boss again knocking at my door, I heard the bells ringing for midnight Mass. . . . I heard the wind howling and the rain beating on the roof. My eyes were closed, but I saw the things in the store-room, the showcase, the dark window, the ikon. The things crowded round me and winked and asked me to let them go home. One after another the strings of the guitar snapped with a whine, snapped endlessly. . . . Through the window looked beggars, old women, prostitutes, waiting for me to open up the shop and give them back their things.

Through my sleep I heard something scratching like a

mouse. It scratched for a long time, monotonously. I turned
over and hunched myself up because of a strong blast of cold
and damp. As I pulled up the bedclothes I heard a rustle
and whispering voices.

What a bad dream! I thought. How uncanny! I wish I
would wake up!

Some glass thing fell and broke. A flame flashed behind
the showcase, and a light played on the ceiling.

'Don't stamp!' a whisper could be heard. 'You'll wake
up that old devil over there. . . . Take off your boots!'

Someone came up to the showcase, looked at me and
touched the padlock. It was a bearded old man, pale and
hollow-cheeked, wearing a torn soldier's great-coat and
shoes tied up with string. He was joined by a tall, thin young
fellow with frightfully long arms, dressed in a shirt which he
wore outside his trousers, and a short, tattered jacket. They
both whispered something, and fiddled about by the showcase.

Burglars! it flashed through my mind.

Although I was asleep I remembered that a revolver
always lay under my pillow. I felt for it quietly, and squeezed
it in my hand. Glass tinkled in the show-case.

'Quiet, you'll wake him! Then we'll have to bump him
off!'

Then I dreamt I gave a loud, wild cry and, frightened by
my own voice, jumped up. The old man and the young
fellow, spreading wide their arms, fell on me, but stepped
backwards on seeing the revolver. I remember, a moment
later they stood before me, pale and tearfully blinking their
eyes, and begged me to let them go. The strong wind came
through the half-broken window and played with the flame
of the candle which the thieves had lit.

'Your honour!' somebody said in a tearful voice from
outside the window. 'Kind sir! Kind friend!'

I looked out of the window and saw the pale, emaciated
face of an old woman, drenched with rain.

'Don't touch them! Let them go!' she wept, looking at me with beseeching eyes. 'Why, it's poverty!'

'Poverty!' repeated the old man.

'Poverty!' sang the wind.

My heart ached, and I pinched myself in order to wake up. . . . But instead of waking up I stood by the showcase, took the things out of it, and convulsively pushed them into the pockets of the old man and the lad.

'Take them, quick!' I gasped. 'It's Christmas to-morrow, and you're paupers! Take them!'

When I had crammed the paupers' pockets full, I tied up the remaining valuables in a bundle and flung them to the old woman. Through the window I gave the old woman a fur coat, a bundle with a black suit, the lace chemises, and the guitar into the bargain. What odd dreams one does have! Then, I remember, the door creaked. The boss, constables and police officers appeared before me, just as if they had sprung out of the ground. The boss stood beside me, but I went on tying up the bundles, as if I did not see him.

'What are you doing, you scoundrel?'

'It's Christmas to-morrow,' I answered. 'They must have something to eat.'

Here the curtain falls, and when it rises again it does so on a new setting. I am no longer in the store-room, but in some other place. A policeman comes up to me, gives me a jug of water for the night, and mutters: 'You're a one, you are! What a thing to try to do on Christmas Eve!' When I woke up it was already light. The rain was no longer beating against the window, the wind was not howling. Bright sunshine was playing gaily on the wall. The first to give me the compliments of the season was a police officer.

'And a happy house-warming to you . . .' he added.

I was tried a month later. For what? I assured the judges that it had been a dream, that it was unfair to try a man for a nightmare. Judge for yourselves—could I have given other peoples' belongings to robbers and scoundrels for no reason at all? And besides, who has ever heard of pawned things being given back without being redeemed first? But the court took my dream for reality, and sentenced me. I am a convict, as you see. Couldn't you put in a word for me somewhere, your honour? I'm not guilty, honest to God I'm not.

OUT OF SHEER BOREDOM

A Holiday Love Story

�֎

NIKOLAI ANDREYEVICH KAPITONOV, a lawyer, had his dinner, finished his cigar and went up to his bedroom to have a rest. He lay down, covered himself with a piece of muslin to keep off mosquitoes, and shut his eyes, but could not go to sleep. The onion he had had in his soup gave him such heartburn that sleep was out of the question.

'No,' he decided after turning over from one side to another half a dozen times, 'I'll never fall asleep to-day. Let's have a look at the papers.'

Nikolai Andreyevich got up, threw a dressing-gown over his shoulders and went, in his stockinged feet, to his study to get the newspapers. He could have no intimation that a sight was awaiting him in the study, far more interesting than heartburn and newspapers.

As he crossed the threshold of the study, the following picture met his gaze: half-lying on a plush-covered sofa, with her feet on a little foot-stool, was his wife, Anna Semyonovna, a lady of thirty-three; her careless and languid pose resembled that in which Cleopatra of Egypt is usually depicted in the act of applying poisonous snakes to herself. The Kapitonovs' tutor, Vanya Stchupaltsev, a first-year engineering student, pink, clean-shaven, aged about nineteen or twenty, was kneeling by her side on one knee. The meaning of this *tableau vivant* was not difficult to grasp: just before the lawyer came in, the lips of the youth and the lady had fused in a long-drawn-out, sultry and languorous kiss.

Nikolai Andreyevich stopped dead in his tracks, held his

106

breath and waited for what would happen next, but could not contain himself and coughed. At that the engineering student looked round and seeing the lawyer, was seized with a momentary paralysis, then blushed, jumped up and ran out of the study. Anna Semyonovna looked embarrassed.

'Char-ming! Sweet!' began the husband, bowing and spreading his arms, 'Congratulations! Sweet and lovely!'

'It's sweet of you, too, to eavesdrop!' mumbled Anna Semyonovna, trying to regain her composure.

'*Merci!* Wonderful!' continued the lawyer, grinning broadly. 'It's all so nice, old dear, that I'd give a hundred roubles to see it again.'

'There was absolutely nothing. . . . You just thought. . . . Silly, even. . . .'

'All right, but who was kissing?'

'We were kissing, that's true, but as to anything more. . . . I cannot follow what you mean.'

Nikolai Andreyevich smiled ironically at his wife's embarrassed expression and shook his head.

'So you've developed a taste for fresh cucumbers in your old age, eh!' he began in a sing-song voice. 'Tired of sturgeon, so it's sardines you want. You have no sense of shame! However, it's natural, I suppose! A Balzac'ian age! There's nothing can be done about it! I understand! I understand and sympathise!'

Nikolai Andreyevich sat down by the window and drummed with his fingers on the window-sill.

'And carry on in the same way . . .' he said with a yawn.

'Don't be silly!' said Anna Semyonovna.

'The weather's damn hot! You ought to have ordered some lemonade or something. Yes, madam, I understand and sympathise. All these kisses, moans and sighs—oh, the heartburn!—it's all sweet and lovely, only you should not turn a boy's head, old dear. You shouldn't, you know. He is a nice, kind boy . . . a good brain and worthy of a better fate. You ought to have pity on him.'

'You don't understand anything. The boy fell head over heels in love with me, and I wanted to give him this pleasure. I allowed him to kiss me.'

'Fell in love . . .' mocked Nikolai Andreyevich. 'You must have laid a hundred snares and mouse traps for him before he fell in love.'

The lawyer yawned and stretched.

'An extraordinary thing!' he grumbled, looking out of the window. 'If I were to kiss a girl as innocently as you have just done, I'd have God knows what heaped on my head: Villain! Seducer! Corrupter! But you, Balzac'ian ladies, you always get away with it. They mustn't put onion in the soup next time, or I shall die of heartburn. . . . Ugh! Quick, look at the object of your love! Running along the drive, the poor mutt, like a scalded cat, without looking back. Imagines, I suppose, that I'll challenge him to a duel for the sake of a treasure such as you. Lecherous as a cat and timid as a hare. You wait, you mutt, I'll give you a fright! You'll be running about all right!'

'Oh, no, please don't say anything to him!' said Anna Semyonovna. 'Don't give him a dressing down, he's not to blame in the slightest.'

'I won't give him a dressing down, only just like that . . . for fun.'

The lawyer yawned, collected the newspapers, picked up the skirts of his dressing-gown, and wandered off to his bedroom. Nikolai Andreyevich lay on the bed for about an hour-and-a-half, read all the newspapers, then dressed and went out for a walk. He walked round the garden cheerfully whisking his cane, but on catching sight of Stchupaltsev some distance off, he folded his arms, frowned and strode on like a provincial tragedian getting ready to meet his rival. Stchupaltsev was sitting on a bench under an ash and, pale and trembling, was preparing for a difficult explanation. He was trying to be brave, wore a grave expression, but was twisting himself into knots, as the saying goes. On seeing the lawyer, he grew even paler, heaved a deep sigh and meekly tucked his feet under the bench. Nikolai Andreyevich came up to him sideways, stood for a bit in silence, and, without looking at him, began:

'Of course, my dear sir, you know what I want to talk to you about. After what I have seen we can no longer remain friends. No, indeed! Emotion makes it difficult for me to speak . . . but you will understand without any words from me that you and I cannot live under the same roof. It is you or I!'

'I understand you,' muttered the student, breathing heavily.

'This villa belongs to my wife, and you, therefore, will remain here, and I . . . I'll go. I have not come here to reproach you, oh no! Reproaches and tears will not bring back what has been irretrievably lost. I have come to ask you what your intentions are. . . . (Pause.) Of course it is no business of mine to interfere in your private affairs, but you must agree that the desire to know about the future fate of a woman so passionately loved is not something you can interpret as interference. Do you intend to live with my wife?'

'But, how do you mean?' said the engineer, abashed, and tucking his feet even further under the bench. 'I . . . I don't know. It's all rather strange.'

'I see you are trying to evade giving a straight answer,' growled the lawyer sullenly. 'Well then, let me tell you straight out: either you take the woman you have seduced and provide her with the necessary means of existence, or else we have a duel. Love creates certain responsibilities, my dear sir, and as a man of honour you must see this! I am going in a week's time, and Anna and the family will come under your wing. I'll pay a certain regular sum for the upkeep of the children.'

'If Anna Semyonovna so wishes,' mumbled the young man. 'I . . . I, as a man of honour, I'll assume . . . but I'm poor, you know! Although. . . .'

'You are a man of honour!' said the lawyer in a hoarse voice, shaking the engineer's hand. 'Thank you! Anyway, I'm giving you a week for reflection. Think it over!'

The lawyer sat down by the side of the engineer and covered his face with his hands.

'But what have you done to me!' he moaned. 'You have shattered my life . . . you have taken away the woman I loved more than life. Oh no, I shall not survive this blow!'

The young man looked at him with anguish and scratched his forehead. He was frightened.

'You have yourself to blame, Nikolai Andreich!' he said with a sigh. 'It's no use crying over spilt milk. Remember, you married Anna entirely for her money . . . then all your life you failed to understand her, tyrannised over her . . . disregarded the purest, noblest impulses of her heart.'

'She told you that?' asked Nikolai Andreyevich, suddenly taking his hands away from his face.

'She did. I know the whole of her life, and . . . and believe me, I became fond not so much of the woman in her as of the martyr.'

'You are a man of honour . . .' sighed the lawyer, getting up. 'Good-bye and be happy. I hope that all that has been said here will remain between us.'

Nikolai Andreyevich heaved another sigh and strode homeward.

Half-way to the house he met Anna Semyonovna.

'Looking for your mutt are you?' he asked. 'Go and have a look the way I made him sweat! . . . So you've had time to make a confession to him! Strange ways you have, you Balzac'ian ladies, I must say! Can't use beauty and freshness as a bait, so you come up with confessions and pathetic little speeches! Stuffed him up with lies, you have! I married for money and I never understood you and I've tyrannised over you and this and that and a damn sight more. . . .'

'I never said anything to him!' exclaimed Anna Semyonovna, blushing crimson.

'All right, all right. . . . I'm being understanding, don't you know, putting myself in your place. Only I'm sorry for the boy. Such a nice boy, honest, sincere.

When evening came and twilight shrouded the earth, the lawyer went for another walk. It was a glorious evening. The trees were sleeping and looked as if no storm could wake them from their young, springtime slumber. The drowsy stars looked down on the earth. Frogs croaked and an owl screeched somewhere behind the garden. The short, jerky whistles of a nightingale's song could be heard from afar.

As he was passing under a spreading lime tree in the dark, Nikolai Andreyevich stumbled on Stchupaltsev.

'Why are you standing here?' he asked.

'Nikolai Andreyevich!' began Stchupaltsev, his voice trembling with emotion. 'I agree to all your conditions, but . . . it's all so strange, somehow. Here you are unhappy all of a sudden . . . you suffer and say that your life is shattered.'

'Yes. What then?'

'If you feel that you have been wronged, well then . . . then I can give you satisfaction, even though I do not believe in duels. If a duel will ease your mind however slightly, I can assure you, I am ready . . . a hundred duels if need be. . . .'

The lawyer laughed and put an arm round the student's waist.

'There, there . . . enough of that! I was only being funny, my dear chap!' he said. 'That is all rot and nonsense. That trashy, contemptible woman is not worth you wasting your words on and getting excited about. Enough, young man! Let us go for a walk.'

'I . . . I don't understand you. . . .'

'There is nothing to understand. A trashy, bad bit of fluff—that's all she is! You have no taste, my dear chap. Why have you stopped? Surprised I am saying things like

9

that about my wife? Of course I shouldn't be saying this to you, but as you are in a way an interested party, it is no use concealing things from you. I'm telling you frankly: drop it! The game's not worth the candle! She told you nothing but lies, and as a "martyr" she isn't worth a farthing. A hysterical Balzac'ian lady. Stupid and tells a lot of lies. I give you my word, my dear chap! I'm being serious. . . .'

'But she is your wife!' said the student in surprise.

'Agreed! I was the same as you and got married, and now would be glad to get unmarried, but—woa! . . . Drop it, my dear fellow! It's not love, only mischief and boredom. If you want to flirt, well then there's Nastya just coming. . . . Hullo, Nastya, where are you going to?'

'To get some *kvas*, sir!' they heard a woman's voice.

'I can understand that,' continued the lawyer, 'but all these hysterical women, martyrs . . . to hell with them! Nastya is a fool, but at least she has no pretensions. . . . Shall we go on?'

The lawyer and the student came out of the garden, glanced back, both heaved a sigh, and went through the field.

A DISAGREEABLE EXPERIENCE

❋

'CABBY, you've a heart of stone. You've never been in love, my man, so you can't understand my psychology. This rain can no more put out the fire in my heart than the fire-brigade can put out the sun. Damn it, how poetically I do express myself! You're not a poet by any chance, are you, cabby?'

'No, sir!'

'Well, you see. . . .'

After groping in his pocket for it for some time Jirkov at last found his purse and began to settle with the driver.

'We agreed, my friend, on one rouble, twenty-five copecks. Receive your fee. Here's a rouble for you, and here's thirty copecks. . . . Five copecks tip. . . . Farewell, and remember me. But first take this basket and put it in the porch. Carefully now, the basket contains the evening-dress of the woman I love more than life itself.'

The driver sighed and reluctantly climbed off the box. After trying to keep his balance in the dark as he splashed through the mud, he succeeded in getting the basket to the front door, and put it down on the steps.

'What weather!' he grumbled reproachfully; and grunting and sighing, he reluctantly clambered back on the box, sniffing as he did so.

He clicked his tongue, and his little horse splashed off through the mud with some hesitation.

'I think I've got everything I need with me,' reflected Jirkov as he felt with his hand along the door-post, searching for the bell. 'Nadya asked me to go to the dress-shop and fetch a dress—I've got it; she asked for sweets and cheese—

I've got them; flowers—I've got them. "All hail thou dwelling chaste . . ." ' he sang. 'But where's the bell, damn it?'

Jirkov was in the complacent mood of a man who has just had supper, who has had a good many drinks, and who knows perfectly well that he will not have to get up early the next day. Moreover, after an hour and half's drive from town through mud and rain, warmth and a young woman were awaiting him. . . . It is pleasant to be chilled and soaked if you know that you will soon get warm again.

Jirkov caught hold of the bell-button in the dark and pushed it twice. He could hear footsteps behind the door.

'Is that you, Dmitri Grigorich?' asked a female whisper.

'It's me, entrancing Dunyasha!' answered Jirkov. 'Open the door quickly, or I shall be soaked to the skin!'

'Oh, my goodness!' whispered Dunyasha, the maid, anxiously, as she opened the door. 'Don't talk so loud and don't make a noise with your feet. The master has arrived from Paris, you know! He came back this evening!'

At the words 'the master' Jirkov backed away from the door, and for a moment was gripped by cowardice and a purely boyish terror, such as even very brave men experience when they are unexpectedly confronted with the possibility of meeting the husband.

What a to do! he thought, as he listened to Dunyasha closing the door very carefully and going back along the passage. What is this? Does it mean I must retrace my steps? Thanks very much, that's a bit unexpected!

And he suddenly thought it funny and amusing. His journey from town to country house to see *her*, in the dead of night and in torrential rain, seemed to him an amusing adventure; and now that he had run into her husband the adventure seemed to him even more curious.

'A most entertaining business, it really is!' he said to himself aloud. 'Where on earth can I go to now? Shall I drive back?'

It was raining and a strong wind was roaring in the trees, but in the dark neither rain nor trees could be seen. Water babbled in the drains and gutters, and seemed to be chuckling and teasing him maliciously. The porch in which Jirkov was standing had no roof, so that he really was getting drenched.

He would come in weather like this, he thought, laughing. The devil take all husbands!

His love-affair with Nadejda Osipovna had started a month ago, but he did not yet know her husband. He only knew that her husband was a Frenchman by origin, that his surname was Boisot, and that by profession he was a dealer. Judging from the photograph which Jirkov had seen, he was a hefty bourgeois of about forty with a moustache and a typical French soldier's face; looking at it one wanted, for some reason, to give the moustache and the little Napoleon beard a tug and ask: 'Well, what's the news, monsieur le sergeant?'

Stumbling and splashing through the liquid mud, Jirkov walked a little way away and shouted:

'Cabby! Cabby!'

No answer came.

'Not a voice, not a groan,' muttered Jirkov, groping his way back to the porch. 'I've sent my cabby away, and this isn't the sort of place you'd find a cab in—not even by day. What a fix! I shall have to wait till morning! Oh, damn, the basket will get wet through and the dress'll be spoilt. It cost two hundred roubles!! What a situation to be in!'

While he was thinking out where he and his basket could shelter from the rain, he remembered that, at the edge of the village, there was an open-air dance place and a covered band-stand next to it.

'Shall I make for the band-stand?' he asked himself. 'It's an idea! But can I drag the basket there? It's so cumbersome, damn it. . . . The cheese and the flowers can go to hell!'

He picked up the basket, but then immediately remembered that while he was going to the band-stand the basket would have time to be soaked half a dozen times.

'Oh, what a problem!' he laughed. 'Lord, the water's gone down my neck! Brrr. . . . Soaked, chilled, drunk, no cab . . . it only remains for the husband to jump out into the street and give me a sound beating with his stick. But what am I to do? I can't stand here all night, and anyway the dress would be ruined. . . . I know. . . . I'll ring again and give the things to Dunyasha, and then I'll go to the band-stand.'

Jirkov rang cautiously. A moment later he could hear steps behind the door and a light flashed through the key-hole.

'Oo ees zaire?' asked a raucous male voice with a foreign accent.

Heavens, it must be her husband, thought Jirkov. I must concoct some story. . . .

'Excuse me, do the Zlyuchkins live here?' he asked.

'Zaire aren't any Zlyushkins here, damn you. Go to hell, you and your Zlyushkins!'

For some reason Jirkov felt embarrassed, gave a guilty cough, and left the porch. As he stepped into a puddle and filled his galosh with water he spat angrily, but then immediately began to laugh again. At every turn his adventure was becoming more and more odd. He took great pleasure in thinking of how the next day he would describe his adventure to his friends and to Nadya herself, how he would imitate her husband's voice and the squelching of his own galoshes. . . . His friends would certainly split their sides with laughter.

There's only one bad thing: the dress will get soaked! he thought. If it wasn't for the dress I'd have been asleep in that band-stand long ago.

He sat down on the basket to shield it from the rain, but more water fell from his soaked cape and hat than did from the sky.

'Oh, damn it!'

When he had been standing in the rain for half an hour he remembered his health.

That's the way to catch a fever, I'm afraid, he thought. What an extraordinary situation! Shall I ring again? Eh? I'll ring, yes I think I will. . . . If her husband opens the door, then I'll cook up some lie and give him the dress. . . . After all, I can't sit here till morning! Well, come what may! Ring!

Full of school-boy cheek, Jirkov put out his tongue at the door and the darkness, and pushed the button. A minute's silence followed; he pushed it again.

'Oo eez zaire?' asked an angry voice with a foreign accent.

'Does Madame Boisot live here?' asked Jirkov in a respectful tone of voice.

'Eh? What the devil d'you want?'

'Madame Katish the dressmaker has sent a dress to Madame Boisot. I'm sorry that it's so late, but Madame Boisot wanted the dress to be sent as soon as possible . . . by the morning. . . . I left town in the evening, but . . . it's shocking weather. . . . I could hardly get here. . . . I didn't. . . .'

Jirkov did not finish what he was saying because the door opened in front of him, and on the threshold, in the swaying light of the lamp, appeared Monsieur Boisot—precisely the same as he was on the photograph, with a soldier's face and a long moustache; however, in the photograph he was portrayed as a dandy, whereas now he was wearing nothing but a night-shirt.

'I wouldn't have bothered you,' Jirkov continued, 'but Madame Boisot asked for the dress to be sent as quickly as possible. I'm Madame Katish's brother . . . and . . . and besides, the weather's shocking.'

'Very good,' said Boisot sullenly, his eyebrows twitching as he took the basket. 'I sank your sister. My vife she vaited for zee dress till after tvelve. Some monsieur had promised to bring it 'er.'

'And would you be so kind as to give your wife the cheese and flowers which she forgot at Madame Katish's?'

Boisot took the cheese and flowers, sniffed both of them and, without closing the door, stood still as if expecting something. He looked at Jirkov, and Jirkov looked at him. A minute passed in silence. Jirkov remembered his friends to whom he would recount his adventure the next day, and felt a desire to play some silly joke as the finishing touch to the whole odd business. But he could not think of a joke, while the Frenchman was standing and waiting for him to go.

'It's dreadful weather,' muttered Jirkov. 'Dark, dirty and wet. I'm soaked through.

'Yes, monsieur, you are quite vet.'

'And what's more, my cabby is gone. I don't know where to go. It would be very kind of you if you would let me stay here in the hall for a bit, until the rain stops.'

'Eh bien, monsieur, take off your galoshes and come here. That's all right, you can.'

The Frenchman closed the door and led Jirkov into a small drawing-room with which he was very familiar. Nothing was changed in the room, except that there was a bottle of red wine on the table, and that on some chairs, which were arranged in a row in the middle of the room, lay a very skimpy, narrow little mattress.

'It's cold,' said Boisot, putting the lamp on the table. 'I only arrived from Paris yesterday. Everyvere it's fine and varm, but here in Russia it's cold and these moustiquos . . . mistiquos . . . les cousins. Zey bite like 'ell.'

Boisot poured out half a glass of wine, made a very angry face, and drank.

'I haven't slept all night,' he said, sitting down on the little mattress. 'Les cousins, and then some svine kept on ringing and asking for Zlyushkin.'

The Frenchman fell silent and dropped his head, presumably waiting for the rain to stop. Jirkov decided that good manners required that he should make conversation.

'You must have been in Paris at a very interesting time,' he said. 'Boulanger retired while you were there.

Jirkov went on talking about Grévy, Déroulède, Zola, and discovered that the Frenchman was hearing all these names for the first time. In Paris Boisot knew only a few business firms, his aunt Madame Blessor, and not another soul. The conversation about politics and literature ended with Boisot once more making an angry face, drinking some wine, and lying down full length on his skimpy mattress.

Well, this husband's rights can't be particularly extensive, thought Jirkov. The mattress is like nothing on earth!

The Frenchman closed his eyes; when he had lain there quietly for a quarter of an hour he suddenly jumped up, fixed his leaden eyes dully on his guest, as if in complete lack of comprehension, then once more made an angry face and drank some wine.

'Zese damned moustiques,' he grumbled, and rubbing one hairy leg against the other, he went out of the room.

Jirkov heard him waking someone up and saying:

'Il y a là un monsieur roux qui t'a apporté une robe.'

Soon he returned and once more applied himself to the bottle.

'My vife she just coming,' he said, yawning. 'I understand, you vant some money?

From bad to worse, thought Jirkov. It's very odd! Nadejda Osipovna will appear in a moment. Of course, I shall pretend that I don't know her.

The rustle of a skirt was heard, the door opened slightly, and Jirkov saw a familiar curly head, cheeks, and sleepy eyes.

'Who is it from—Madame Katish?' asked Nadejda Osipovna, but immediately afterwards, recognising Jirkov, she gave a cry, laughed and came into the room.

'It's you?' she asked. 'What's all this pretence for? But how did you get so muddy?'

Jirkov blushed, put on a stern expression, and at a complete loss as to how to behave, looked askance at Boisot.

'Oh, I understand!' guessed the lady. 'You were probably frightened of Jacques? I forgot to warn Dunyasha. . . . Do you know each other? This is my husband, Jacques, and this is Stepan Andreich. . . . You brought the dress? Well, merci, my friend. . . . Come, or else I shall fall asleep. Sleep well, Jacques . . .' she said to her husband. 'You're tired after your journey.'

Jacques looked at Jirkov in amazement, shrugged his shoulders, and with an angry expression reached for the bottle. Jirkov also shrugged his shoulders, and followed Nadejda Osipovna.

.   .   .   .   .

He looked at the dull sky and at the muddy road, and thought:

How dirty! What strange places an intelligent man can get to!

And he thought of morality and immorality, of cleanliness and uncleanliness. As often happens to people who find themselves in some evil place, he remembered nostalgically both his study and the papers on his desk, and he longed to go home.

He walked quietly through the drawing-room, past the sleeping Jacques.

He was silent all the way home, tried not to think of Jacques, who for some reason he could not get out of his head, and no longer talked to the cabby. His heart was as upset as his stomach.

HIS FIRST APPEARANCE

※

PYATERKIN, a junior barrister, was returning in a simple peasant cart from the small provincial town of N——, where he had gone to defend a shopkeeper on a charge of arson. In his heart of hearts he felt more depressed than he had ever been. Humiliation, failure and insult had, he felt, been heaped upon him. He felt that that day, the day of his first appearance in court for which he had waited so long and from which he had expected so much, had entirely ruined his career, his faith in mankind and his conception of the world.

To begin with, the accused had shamelessly and cruelly deceived him. Before the trial the shopkeeper had blinked his eyes in such obvious sincerity and had so frankly and simply protested his innocence that, in the eyes of a psychologist and physiognomist (both of which the young lawyer considered himself to be) all evidence against him appeared shamelessly far-fetched, mere fault-finding and prejudice. But at the trial itself the shopkeeper had turned out to be a swindler and a scoundrel, and the wretched psychology went to hell.

Secondly, it seemed to him that his, Pyaterkin's, behaviour at the trial had been impossible. He had stuttered, had muddled his questions, had stood up in front of witnesses and flushed stupidly. His tongue had altogether refused to obey him and had stumbled in ordinary speech as if it had been trying to get round a tongue-twister. He had spoken desultorily, as if in a coma, looking over the heads of the jury. And as he spoke he had the impression that the jury were looking at him with derision and contempt.

In the third place, and worst of all, both the public prosecutor, an old, experienced lawyer, and the opposing barrister had behaved in an unfriendly way. He had the impression that they had agreed beforehand to ignore counsel for the defence, and if they did glance up at him it was only to make him the butt of their off-handedness, to scoff at him and to make a brilliant repartee at his expense. Irony and condescension were apparent in their speeches. As they spoke they gave the impression of apologising for the fact that counsel was such an innocent little nincompoop. Finally, Pyaterkin could bear it no longer. During the interval he rushed up to the opposing barrister and, trembling in every limb, reeled off a lot of rude remarks. Then, when the session was over, he caught up with the public prosecutor on the staircase and gave him a piece of his mind too.

Fourthly. . . . But the enumeration of all that was troubling our hero and gnawing at his vitals would need a 'fifthly', a 'sixthly' and so on inclusive of 'in the hundredth place'. . . .

It's a disgrace . . . it's abominable! he thought, as he sat in the cart, with his ears sunk in his collar, eating his heart out. Finished! To hell with the bar! I'll go and hide myself in the backwoods, I'll go into seclusion . . . as far as possible from these gentlemen . . . as far as possible from these squabbles! 'Get a move on, damn you!' he turned on the driver. 'You're not driving a corpse to its wedding! Go on, faster!'

'Faster . . . faster!' mimicked the driver. 'Can't you see what the road's like? Would tire the devil out if you tried to make *him* go faster. This weather's sheer punishment, God knows!'

The weather was abominable. It seemed to share Pyaterkin's indignation, hatred and suffering. It was as dark as soot and a cold, damp wind blew and whistled on every note. The rain was pouring down. A mixture of snow and sticky mud squelched underneath the wheels. Gullies and potholes and little bridges, half washed away, succeeded each other without end.

'Can't see a thing . . .' continued the driver. 'Shan't get there by morning at this rate. We'll have to spend the night at Luke's.'

'Who's Luke?'

'An old man who lives further along the road in the wood here. He's taken the forester's place. Ah, there's his cottage.'

They could hear the hoarse barking of dogs, and a dim light flickered through the naked branches.

If ever on a dark and rainy night you see a light in a wood, you are sure to feel a desire for company however misanthropic you may be. And so it was with Pyaterkin. When the cart stopped at the cottage with the light welcoming them shyly through the single small window, he felt better.

'Good evening, grand-dad!' he said kindly to Luke, who was standing in the passage just inside the cottage and was scratching his belly with both hands. 'May we spend the night here?'

'You m . . . may,' growled Luke. 'There are two others here as it is. . . . Come into the living-room, please.'

Pyaterkin stooped, stepped into the living-room and . . . his misanthropy came back with a vengeance. At a small table lit up by a tallow candle sat the two men who had had such a powerful influence on his mood: von Pach, the public prosecutor, and Semechkin the opposing barrister. Like Pyaterkin, they too had been returning from N——, and like him had landed up at Luke's. On seeing counsel for the defence coming in, they were both pleasantly surprised, and jumped up.

'Hullo! How did you get here?' they began. 'The bad weather has driven you in here as well? Welcome! Do come and sit with us!'

Pyaterkin had thought that as soon as they saw him they would turn away in awkward silence, and therefore interpreted this friendly welcome at best as insolence.

'I don't understand,' he muttered, shrugging his shoulders with dignity. 'After what has passed between us, I . . . I am even surprised!'

Von Pach looked at Pyaterkin in surprise, shrugged his shoulders and, turning to Semechkin, continued the interrupted conversation:

'Well, I was reading the report . . . and you know, old boy, that report was just a mass of contradictions. . . . The police inspector wrote for instance, that the deceased woman Ivanova was dead drunk when she left the party and died after she had gone two miles on foot. How could she have gone two miles on foot if she had been dead drunk? Now, isn't that a contradiction? Eh?'

While von Pach was thus perorating, Pyaterkin sat down on a bench and began to examine his temporary abode. . . . A light in a wood is romantic only at a distance—at close quarters it is sorry prose. . . . Here it lit up a small, grey cubby-hole of a room with slanting walls and a sooty ceiling. In the corner on the right hung a dark ikon, in the corner on the left stood a clumsy-looking stove, gloomy and for all the world like a tree with a hollow in it. On the ceiling a long pole, from which a cradle must once have hung, was stretched across the rafters. A ramshackle table and two narrow, rickety benches made up all the furniture. It was dark, stuffy and cold. There was a smell of rot and burnt candle grease.

The swine . . . thought Pyaterkin with a sidelong glance at his enemies. They've insulted a man, trampled him in the mire, and now they're carrying on a conversation as if nothing had happened! 'I say,' he turned to Luke. 'Have you got another room by any chance? I can't stay here.'

'There's the passage, but it's cold there, sir.'

'Damned cold . . .' growled Semechkin, 'had I known I'd have brought drinks and cards with me. Shall we have some tea, what do you think? Heat us up a samovar, granddad!'

Half an hour later Luke served up a dirty samovar, a tea-pot with a broken spout and three cups.

'I have some tea . . .' said von Pach. 'All we want now is sugar. . . . Give us some sugar, grand-dad!'

'Mercy on us! Sugar!' said Luke, who was standing in the passage grinning. 'You want sugar right in the middle of the forest! You're not in town, you know!'

'All right then, let's drink it without sugar,' von Pach decided.

Semechkin made the tea and poured out three cups.

They've poured some out for me as well . . . thought Pyaterkin. I don't want their tea! Spit in my face and then offer me tea! They simply have no self-respect, these people. I'll ask Luke to give me another cup and I'll just drink hot water. Besides, I've got some sugar.

Luke did not have a fourth cup. Pyaterkin poured the tea out of the third cup, filled it up again with hot water and began to sip it, giving an occasional bite at the sugar. Hearing the loud scrunching, his enemies exchanged glances and burst out laughing.

'It's delightful, honestly!' prattled on von Pach. 'We have no sugar, he has no tea. . . . Ha-ha. . . . Gay, isn't it! What a child he still is. A great lout like that, and yet he's kept himself young enough to be able to sulk like a school-girl. . . . Here, my friend!' he said, turning to Pyaterkin. 'You shouldn't snub our tea. . . . It isn't one of the cheaper sort. . . . And if you don't drink it because you're too proud, remember you could pay for the tea with your sugar.'

Pyaterkin made no answer.

Cads . . . he thought. They've insulted me and slandered me, and now they're trying to thrust their friendship on me. And these are known as humans! It means they simply don't care about all the ruderies I told them after the trial. . . . I shan't pay any attention to them. . . . I'll lie down.

A sheepskin coat was stretched out on the floor next to the stove. . . . At the head of it lay a long bolster filled with straw. . . . Pyaterkin stretched himself out on the sheepskin coat, put his burning head on the bolster, and covered himself with his fur coat.

'What a bore!' yawned Semechkin. 'Too cold and dark to read, nowhere to sleep. . . . Brr! . . . Tell me, Osip Osipych, if Luke, say, were to have a dinner in a restaurant and not pay for it, what would that be: larceny or fraud?'

'Neither one nor the other . . . simply a case for civil action. . . .'

An argument started which went on for an hour and a half; Pyaterkin listened and shook with rage. Half a dozen times he was overwhelmed with the desire to jump up and join in the argument.

What nonsense! he thought, suffering torments as he listened to them. How out of date they are! How illogical!

The argument ended with von Pach lying down next to Pyaterkin, covering himself with his fur coat, and saying:

'That's enough, now. . . . All this arguing of ours is not letting counsel for the defence sleep. Lie down. . . .'

'He's asleep already, I think . . .' said Semechkin, lying down on the other side of Pyaterkin. 'Are you asleep, my friend?'

They can't leave me alone . . . thought Pyaterkin. The swine!

'He doesn't answer, so he must be asleep . . .' muttered von Pach. 'He's managed to fall asleep in this pig-stye. . . . They say lawyers lead an armchair sort of life. . . . It's not an armchair sort of life, it's a dog's life. . . . Just look at this damned place we've landed up in. You know, I rather like our neighbour . . . what's his name? Shestërkin? Full of zeal and fire. . . .'

'Mm, yes. . . . He'll be a good lawyer in a few years' time. . . . He has a way with him, that young man. . . . Hardly out of his nappies, yet he speaks with a flourish and likes letting off fireworks. . . . Only he shouldn't have dragged in Hamlet in his speech.'

The close proximity of his enemies and their cool, indifferent tone were choking Pyaterkin. He was ready to burst from rage and shame.

'And that business with the sugar,' von Pach grinned. 'A regular school-girl! What's he offended with us for? Do you know?'

'I'm damned if I do. . . .'

Pyaterkin could bear it no longer. He jumped up and opened his mouth to say something, but all the suffering he had endured in the course of the day was too much for him: words did not come, but hysterical weeping instead.

'What's the matter with him?' exclaimed von Pach in distress. 'My dear man, what's the matter with you?'

'Are you . . . are you ill?' said Semechkin, jumping up. 'What's the matter with you? Have you got no money? What is it?'

'It's mean . . . vile! The whole day . . . the whole day!'

'My dear boy, what is vile and mean? Osip Osipych, get me some water! My dear fellow, what's the matter? Why are you in such a bad temper to-day? To-day you were probably entrusted with the defence for the first time? Were you? Well then, it's understandable. You have a good cry, my dear fellow. . . . In my day I wanted to go and hang myself, but crying is better than hanging. You cry—you'll feel better.'

'Vile . . . mean!'

'But nothing was vile! It was all as it should have been. You spoke well and you were listened to well. It's over-anxiety, old fellow. I remember the first time I undertook someone's defence. I had brown trousers on and a musician had lent me his miserable-looking tails. There I sat, and thought the public was laughing at my trousers. The accused had fooled me, so it seemed to me, and the prosecutor was making fun of me and anyway I was stupid. I suppose you have decided that the bar can go to hell? This happens to everyone. You are not the first nor the last. One's first appearance in court certainly costs one dear.'

'And who was jeering? Who was making fun of me?'

'Nobody was. You only imagined it. All beginners imagine it. Didn't you think too that the jury was looking at you with contempt? You did? Well, there you are. Have a drink of water, old boy. Cover yourself up.'

Pyaterkin's enemies covered him up with fur coats and looked after him all night as if he were a child. His sufferings of a whole day were nothing but a bubble.

HOLY SIMPLICITY

�֍

FATHER SAVVA JEZLOV, the aged prior of Holy Trinity Church in P——, received an unexpected visit from his son, Alexander, a well-known Moscow lawyer. When the lonely old widower caught sight of his only child, whom he had not seen since he went to the university some twelve or fifteen years before, he grew pale, shook, and stood rooted to the ground. Their joy and delight knew no bounds.

That evening father and son talked. The lawyer ate, drank, and was visibly moved.

'How nice and pleasant it is here,' he said, going into raptures as he fidgeted on his chair. 'It's cosy and warm, and there's a sort of patriarchal smell here. It really is nice!'

Father Savva, obviously giving himself airs in front of the old cook for having such a grown-up and gallant son, walked round the table with his hands behind his back, and tried to make himself appear 'learned' in order to please his guest.

'It's a fact, my boy,' he said. 'It's turned out precisely as I hoped in my heart: both you and I—we both went in for learning. Now you went to the university, and I was educated at the Kiev Academy. . . . So we both followed the same path. . . . We understand each other. . . . Only I don't know what they do in the academies nowadays. In my day they laid great stress on the classics, and even taught ancient Hebrew. What do they do now?'

'Don't know. But you've got marvellous sturgeon, Father. I'm full already, but I'll eat some more all the same.'

'You eat, you eat. You should eat more because you do brain work, not physical work . . . mm . . . not physical work. You're a graduate, you have to use your brains. Are you staying long?'

'I didn't come to stay. I came to see you quite by chance, Father, like a *deus ex machina*. I came here on tour, to defend your ex-mayor. . . . You probably know there's to be a trial here to-morrow.'

'I see. So you're presumably in the legal profession? A lawyer?'

'Yes, I'm a barrister.'

'I see. May God give you His blessing. What's your rank?'

'Honestly, I don't know, Father.'

I'd like to ask about his salary, thought Father Savva, But they think a question like that is indiscreet. Judging by his clothes and by that gold watch there, I should think he must get more than a thousand roubles.

The old man and the lawyer fell silent.

'I didn't know you had such sturgeon, or I'd have come to see you last year,' the son said. 'I wasn't far from here last year, in your provincial capital. What funny towns you have here!'

'That's just what they are . . . funny . . . nothing in them!' Father Savva agreed. 'Nothing to be done! They're far away from intellectual centres . . . steeped in prejudice. Civilisation hasn't seeped through to them yet. . . .'

'That's not the point. . . . You just listen to a funny story that happened to me. While I was in your provincial capital, I went to the theatre. I asked for a ticket at the box-office, but they said to me: There will be no performance, because not a single ticket has been sold yet! So I asked them: what are your takings if there's a full house? They said: three hundred roubles! So I said: tell them to put the show on, I'll pay three hundred. . . . I paid three hundred roubles because I was bored, but when I began to watch their harrowing drama, I was even more bored. . . . Ha-ha. . . .'

Father Savva glanced incredulously at his son, glanced at the cook, and sniggered behind his hand.

What a fib! he thought. 'Where did you get those three hundred roubles from, Sashenka?' he asked timidly.

'What d'you mean, where from? From my pocket, of course. . . .'

'Mm . . . forgive me for an indiscreet question, but what salary do you get?'

'It depends. . . . One year I would earn about thirty thousand, another year I don't even scrape up twenty thousand. . . . Years vary.'

What a fib! Ho-ho-ho! What a fib! . . . thought Father Savva, roaring with laughter and looking lovingly at his son's somewhat drunken face. How youth does brag! Ho-ho-ho! Thirty thousand—he certainly lays it on a bit thick! 'It's incredible, Sashenka!' he said. 'I'm sorry, but . . . ho-ho-ho . . . thirty thousand! One could build two houses with that amount of money. . . .'

'Don't you believe me?'

'It's not that I don't believe you exactly, but . . . how shall I express it. . . . You're awfully sort of . . . er . . . ho-ho-ho. . . . Well, if you get such a lot of money, what do you do with it all?'

'I spend it, Father. . . . Life in the capital simply eats up money. For every thousand you spend here you have to spend five there. I keep horses, play cards . . . sometimes I go out on the spree.'

'I see. . . . But you should save!'

'Can't be done. . . . Haven't got the right kind of nerves for saving. . . .' (The lawyer sighed.) 'There's nothing to be done with me. Last year I bought myself a house on the Polyanka for sixty thousand. After all, it might be a help in my old age! And what d'you think? Less than two months after I'd bought it, I had to mortgage it. I mortgaged it, and all the cash went—pouf! I lost some of it at cards, and some of it went on drink.'

'Ho-ho-ho! He's fibbing, he is!' the old man tittered. 'How amusingly he fibs!'

'I'm not fibbing, Father.'

'But you can't lose a house at cards or through drink.'

'You can drink away not only a house, but the whole globe! To-morrow I'll take five thousand away from here, but I've a feeling that these five thousand won't get me as far as Moscow. It's the planetoid I was born under.'

'Not planetoid, planet,' Father Savva corrected him, then coughed and looked with dignity at the old cook. 'I'm sorry, Sashenka, but I doubt what you say. Why, what do you get such sums for?'

'For my talent. . . .'

'Mm. . . . Perhaps you do get about three thousand, but as to thirty thousand or, let's say, buying houses, I'm sorry, . . . I have my doubts. But let's drop this argument. Now tell me, how are things in Moscow? Gay, I suppose? Have you a lot of friends?'

'A great many. The whole of Moscow knows me.'

'Ho-ho-ho! He's fibbing, he is! Ho-ho! All these wonders you're telling me, my boy!'

Father and son went on conversing in this way for a long time. The lawyer also told him about his marriage (with a dowry of forty thousand roubles), he described his journeys to Nijni Novgorod, and his divorce which cost him ten thousand roubles. The old man listened, gasped, and roared with laughter.

'He's fibbing, he is! Ho-ho-ho! Why, Sashenka, I never knew you had such a gift of the gab! Ho-ho-ho! I'm not saying that as a reproach. I enjoy listening to you. Go on, go on.'

'But I've been talking too much,' said the lawyer at last, getting up from the table. 'The trial's to-morrow, and I haven't read the case yet. Good night.'

When he had taken his son to his own room Father Savva abandoned himself to delight.

'You saw what he's like, eh? You did?' he whispered to the cook. 'That's what he is. . . . A university man, a humanist, emancipated, but not ashamed to visit his old man. Forgot his father and suddenly remembered him again. Just like that—remembered him again, the old stick-in-the-mud,' he said to himself. 'Ho-ho-ho! He's a good son! A kind son! And did you notice? He treats me as an equal . . . sees a fellow scholar in me. So he understands me, that means. Pity we didn't call the deacon round to have a look at him!'

When he had poured out his soul to the cook, Father Savva went to his bedroom on tiptoe and peeped through the key-hole. The lawyer was lying on the bed smoking a cigar and reading a voluminous note-book. Beside him on a small table stood a bottle of wine, which Father Savva had not previously seen.

'I've just come in for a moment . . . to see if you're comfortable,' mumbled the old man, going into his son's room. 'Comfortable? Is the bed soft enough? Why don't you undress?'

The lawyer gave a grunt and frowned. Father Savva sat at the foot of the bed and was plunged in thought.

'Oh, yes . . .' he began, after a short pause. 'I keep on thinking about all you've said. On the one hand, I'm grateful to you for amusing an old man, but on the other hand, as your father and . . . and an educated man, I can't keep quiet and refrain from passing certain remarks. I know you were joking at dinner, but after all, you know, both science and faith condemn lies even in joke. Hrm. . . . I've got a cough. Hrm. . . . Forgive me, but I'm speaking as a father. Where did you get that wine from?'

'I brought it with me. D'you want some? It's good wine, eight roubles a bottle.'

'Ei-ght? That's a fib, that is!' Father Savva threw up his hands. 'Ho-ho-ho! But why should you pay eight roubles for this? Ho-ho-ho! I'll buy you the very best wine for a rouble! Ho-ho-ho!'

'Well, quick march, old man, you're preventing me from working. So long!'

The old man left the room, tittering and throwing up his

hands, and quietly closed the door behind him. At midnight, when he had read his Breviary and given orders to the cook for the next day's dinner, Father Savva looked into his son's room again.

His son was still reading, drinking and smoking.

'It's time to go to bed . . . get undressed and put out the candle,' the old man said, bringing with him into his son's room a smell of incense and burning candles. 'It's midnight already. . . . Is that your second bottle? Oho!'

'Can't do anything without wine, Father. . . . There can be no work without a stimulant.'

Savva sat down on the bed, was silent for a moment, and then began:

'It's like this, my boy. . . . Mm, yes. . . . I don't know if I'll be alive . . . if I'll see you again, so it's better if I instruct you about my will to-day. . . . You see. . . . During the whole forty years that I've been in orders I've saved up about fifteen hundred roubles. When I die, take it, but. . . .'

Father Savva solemnly blew his nose and continued:

'But don't squander it, keep it. . . . And I'd ask you, after my death, to send a hundred roubles to my niece Varenka. And if you're not short, send Zinaida twenty roubles too. They're orphans.'

'You send them the whole fifteen hundred. . . . I don't need it, Father. . . .'

'You're fibbing?'

'Seriously. . . . I'd just squander it, anyway.'

'Mm. . . . After all, I did save it up!' Savva was offended. 'I put aside every single copeck for you. . . .'

'Well, I'll put your money in a glass case as a sign of parental love, but as I don't need it. . . . Fifteen hundred—pah!'

'Well, as you like. . . . Had I known I wouldn't have saved, wouldn't have been so careful. . . . You go to sleep!'

Father Savva made the sign of the cross over the lawyer

and left the room. He was rather offended. . . . His son's perfunctory and indifferent attitude to his forty years' savings had abashed him. But the feeling of affront and embarrassment soon passed. The old man once again felt an urge to go and chat with his son, to talk 'learnedly' and recall the past, but he could no longer muster sufficient courage to bother the busy lawyer. He walked and walked through the dark rooms, thought and thought, and went into the hall to look at his son's fur coat. Forgetting himself in parental delight, he seized the coat with both hands and hugged and kissed it, and made the sign of the cross over it, as if it was no fur coat, but his own son, the 'university graduate'. Sleep he could not.

THE DIPLOMAT

A Scene

ANNA LVOVNA KUVALDIN, the wife of a principal in the
Civil Service, breathed her last.

Her friends and relations conferred among themselves.
'Well, what's to be done now?' they asked. 'Her husband
should be informed. He loved the dead woman all the same,
even though he didn't live with her. He came to see her the
other day, crawled on his knees to her and kept on saying:
"Annochka, won't you ever forgive me one momentary
impulse?" and other things of the same sort, you know. He
must be told. . . .'

'Aristarkh Ivanych!' a tearful aunt turned to Colonel
Piskarev, who was taking part in the family council. 'You're
Mikhail Petrovich's friend. Do us a favour, go and see him
at the office and tell him about this misfortune. . . .
Only don't tell him all at once, my dear, don't stun him, or
else anything might happen to him. His health's not strong.
Prepare him first, and only then. . . .'

Colonel Piskarev put on his cap and went off to the
head office of the railway where the newly-widowed man
worked. He found him working out a balance sheet.

'Mikhail Petrovich,' he began, sitting down at Kuvaldin's
table and wiping the sweat from his brow. 'Good morning,
old man! Goodness how dusty the streets are! You go on
writing, go on, I won't bother you. . . . I'll sit here a
moment and then go. . . . I was passing by, you know, and
thought: why, this is where Misha works! Let's drop in on
him! Besides, there's also a little matter. . . .'

'Sit down for a bit, Aristarkh Ivanych. . . . Wait a little. . . . I shall be finished in a quarter of an hour, and then we can talk. . . .'

'You go on writing, go on. . . . I just dropped in like that. . . . As I was passing. . . . I'll just say a couple of words and then—off I go!'

Kuvaldin put down his pen and prepared to listen. The colonel scratched himself behind the collar and continued:

'It's stuffy in here, but it's simply heavenly outside. . . . Sunshine, a little breeze, you know . . . birds. . . . Spring, in fact. There I was, going along the street and feeling really fine, you know. . . . I'm an independent man, a widower. . . . I can go wherever I want to. . . . I can go to the pub if I want to, or take a ride in a tram, and there's no-one to stop me, no one to scream at me at home. . . . A bachelor's life, old boy, is the best life in the world. . . . You can do what you like! You're free! You can breathe, and you feel that you do! In a moment I'll go home, and that'll be that. . . . No one will dare ask me where I've been. . . . I'm my own master. . . . You know, old boy, a lot of people praise family life, but in my opinion it's worse than hard labour. . . . All those fashions, bustles, gossip, screaming . . . visitors all the time . . . children crawling into God's world one after another . . . expense . . . faugh!'

'In a minute,' said Kuvaldin, taking up his pen, 'I'll be finished, and then. . . .'

'You go on writing, go on. . . . It's all right if you chance on a wife who doesn't happen to be a devil, but what if she's Satan in skirts? What if she's the sort that jabbers and nags for days on end? . . . Anyone would scream! Why, take yourself for example. . . . While you were single you looked like a man, but as soon as you married you just faded away—always in the dumps, you were. . . . She disgraced you all over town . . . drove you out of the house. . . . Well, what's good about that? You can't pity a wife like that. . . .'

'I was to blame for the break-up of our marriage, not her,' sighed Kuvaldin.

'Oh, drop that, do! I know her! Bad-tempered, self-willed, cunning! Every word a poisoned barb, every look a sharp knife. . . . And she was more spiteful than words can say, the deceased was!'

'What do you mean—"the deceased"?' said Kuvaldin, all round-eyed.

'Why, did I really say "the deceased"?' Piskarev checked himself, blushing. 'I didn't say that at all. . . . What on earth's the matter with you. . . . You've gone quite pale! Ha-ha. . . . You should use your ears!'

'Did you visit Anyuta to-day?'

'I dropped in in the morning. . . . She was in bed. . . . Bullying the servants. . . . This was wrong and that was wrong. . . . An unbearable woman! I don't understand what you love her for, drat her. . . . I wish she'd set you free. . . . You'd live in freedom, enjoy yourself. . . . Marry someone else. . . . All right, all right, I won't say any more! Don't look so cross! I'm only speaking as an old man. . . . You can do what you like so far as I'm concerned. . . . Love her if you want to, or don't . . . but I'm only saying it like that . . . for your own good. . . . She doesn't live with you, doesn't want to know you . . . what sort of a wife is that? She's ugly, sickly, ill-natured. . . . Nothing to regret her for. If only. . . .'

'It's all very well for you to talk, Aristarkh Ivanych!' sighed Kuvaldin. 'But you can't just pull love out, like a hair of your head.'

'But what is there to love! Spite was all she ever gave you. You must forgive me, I'm an old man, but I didn't like her. . . . Couldn't bear her! Whenever I drove past her flat I used to shut my eyes so as not to see her. . . . Oh, it doesn't matter now. God rest her soul and give her peace, but . . . I didn't like her, though it might have been my fault'

'Listen, Aristarkh Ivanych . . .' said Kuvaldin, going pale. 'That's the second time you've let it out. . . . Has she died, or what?'

'What d'you mean, who's died? No one's died, it's just that I didn't like the deceased. . . . Oh, bother, I don't mean the deceased, but what's her name . . . your Annushka. . . .'

'But is she dead, or what? Aristarkh Ivanych, don't torture me! You're somehow strangely excited, talk in a confused way. . . . You sing the praises of a single life. . . . She's dead? Is that it?'

'Hold on, who's dead?' muttered Piskarev, coughing. 'How you do jump to conclusions, old man. . . . And what if she is dead? We'll all die one day, and she'll have to die too like the rest of us. . . . You'll die and I'll die. . . .'

Kuvaldin's eyes reddened and filled with tears.

'At what time?' he asked quietly.

'Not at any time. . . . There you go, snivelling already! But she hasn't died! Who told you that she's died?'

'Aristarkh Ivanych, I . . . I beg you, don't spare me!'

'It doesn't seem to be any use talking to you, old boy, you're just like a child. I never told you that she'd passed on? I never did, did I? What are you slobbering about then? You go and have a look at her—alive and kicking! When I dropped in to see her she was quarrelling with her aunt. . . . There was Father Matvei, saying the Requiem, and she was shouting so the whole house could hear.'

'What Requiem? Why was it being said?'

'What, the Requiem? Oh, just like that . . . kind of instead of Mass. . . . I mean, there wasn't any Requiem, but something . . . there wasn't anything.'

Aristarkh Ivanych was thoroughly muddled. He stood up, turned to face the window and coughed.

'I've got a cough, old man. . . I don't know where I can have caught it. . . .'

Kuvaldin got up too, and walked round the table in great agitation.

'You're not being straightforward with me,' he said, pulling at his beard with trembling fingers. 'Now it's clear. . . . It's all clear. What's all this diplomacy for, I'd like to know? Why not say things straight out? She is dead, isn't she?'

'Mm. . . . Well, how shall I put it?' Piskarev shrugged his shoulders. 'Not dead, exactly, but. . . . Now there you are, crying already! After all, we'll all die! She's not the only one to be mortal, we'll all finish up in the next world! Rather than cry in public like that, you'd do better to say a prayer. . . . You might at least make the sign of the cross!

Kuvaldin looked dully at Piskarev for a moment, then turned terribly pale, flopped into an armchair, and broke into hysterical tears. . . . His colleagues leaped up from their places and dashed to his assistance. Piskarev scratched the back of his head and frowned.

'What a business it is, with people like that, honestly!' he grumbled, in despair. 'He's howling—and why's he howling, I ask you? Misha, are you in your right mind? Misha!' he said, nudging Kuvaldin. 'She's not dead yet, I tell you! Who told you she was dead? On the contrary, the doctors say there's hope yet. Misha, hey, Misha! I tell you she's not dead! Would you like us to go and see her together? We'll just get there in time for the Requiem. . . . I mean . . . what am I saying? Not for the Requiem, but for dinner, Mishenka! I assure you, she's still alive! I'll be damned if she isn't! May I be struck dumb! Don't you believe me? Let's go to her, then. . . . You can call me all the names in the world then if. . . . And where could he have got the idea from, I can't understand? I was at the deceased's house today, that's to say, not at the deceased's but. . . . Oh, bother!'

The colonel made a gesture with his hand, gave up, and left

the office. When he arrived back at the dead woman's house he flung himself on the sofa and tore his hair.

'You go and see him yourselves!' he said in despair. 'You prepare him for the news yourselves, but leave me out of it! I don't want to do it! I just said a couple of words to him. . . . I only just gave a slight hint, and you see what's happened to him! In a faint, he is! Dying! I wouldn't do it again for anything in the world! You go yourselves. . . .!'

MUTUAL SUPERIORITY

❉

'Now, *mes enfants*, you must be sure to call on Baroness Scheppling (with two "p's") . . .' my mother-in-law repeated for the hundredth time, as she settled me and my young bride in the carriage. 'The baroness is a very old friend of mine. . . . And while you're about it, go and see General Jerebchikov's wife too . . . she'll be offended if you don't call on her.'

We climbed into the carriage and drove off to pay our first calls after our marriage. It seemed to me that my wife's face adopted a pompous expression, whereas I hung my head and was sunk in melancholy. . . . My wife and I had many dissimilarities, but none of them caused me more spiritual torment than the dissimilarity between our friends and connections. My wife's list of friends shone with a motley assortment of colonels' and generals' wives, Baroness Scheppling (with two 'p's'), Count Derzai-Chertovchinov, and a whole swarm of aristocratic school friends; whereas, on my side, there was nothing but a mass of *mauvais ton*: an uncle who was a retired prison inspector, a cousin who kept a dress-making business, my fellow civil-servants—all drunkards and good-for-nothings, and none of them higher than a principal in the civil service—Plevkov (a merchant), and so on. I felt a sense of shame. To escape ignominy it would have been better not to visit my friends at all, but this would have meant laying up a lot of trouble and bother for myself. My cousin might, perhaps, have been crossed off the list, but the calls on my uncle and on Plevkov were unavoidable. I had borrowed money from my uncle for the wedding expenses, and I owed Plevkov for the furniture.

'Very soon, my sweetie,' said I to my spouse by way of

preparing the ground, 'we shall arrive at my uncle Pupkin's. He's from a very ancient, noble family . . . his uncle was a suffragan in some diocese or other, but he's an eccentric and lives like a pig; I don't mean the vicar lives like a pig, but Pupkin does. . . . I'm taking you there so that you can have a good laugh . . . he's an awful silly ass. . . .'

The carriage stopped outside a small, three-windowed cottage, with grey, rusty shutters. We got out of the carriage and rang the bell. . . . We could hear a dog barking loudly, then a reprimand: 'Sh! Damn you!'—then a yelp, a scuffle behind the door. . . . After a prolonged scuffle the door opened, and we went into the hall. . . . We were met by my cousin Masha, a little girl with a dirty nose, wearing her mother's cardigan. I pretended not to recognise her, and went to the coat-stand where, together with my uncle's fox-fur coat, hung someone's trousers and a starched skirt. I took off my galoshes and gave a furtive look at the drawing-room. There, at the table, sat my uncle in his dressing-gown, and with slippers on his bare feet. The hope that we might not find him at home turned to dust and ashes. . . . Screwing up his eyes and wheezing so that it could be heard all over the house, he was taking orange peel out of a vodka decanter with a piece of wire. He had the preoccupied and concentrated look of an inventor at work. We went in. As soon as he saw us Pupkin became covered with embarrassment, dropped his wire, and gathering up the skirts of his dressing-gown, he dashed out of the room.

'I'm just coming!' he shouted.

'He's taken to flight . . .' I laughed, consumed with shame and afraid to look at my wife. 'Isn't it funny, Sonya? He really is frightfully eccentric. . . . And just look what furniture! A three-legged table, a paralytic piano, a cuckoo-clock. . . . Honestly, it's like prehistoric monsters living here rather than human beings. . . .'

'What's that drawing?' my wife asked, looking at the pictures which were hung pell-mell with photographs.

'That's St. Seraphim feeding a bear in the Sarov hermitage. . . . And that's a portrait of the suffragan, when he was still an inspector in a seminary. . . . Look, you see he's got the order of St. Anne. . . . An estimable man. . . . I . . . .'
(I blew my nose.)

But nothing made me feel so ashamed as the smell. . . . There was a smell of vodka, of bad oranges, of the turpentine with which my uncle defended himself against moth, of coffee grounds—all this together gave out an acutely sour odour. . . . My cousin Mitya, a small school-boy with large, sticking-out ears, came into the room and clicked his heels. . . . When he had picked up the orange peel he took a cushion off the sofa, wiped the dust from the piano with his sleeve, and left the room. . . . He had obviously been sent to 'tidy up'.

'Well, here I am!' said my uncle at last, coming in and buttoning up his waist-coat. 'Well, here I am! I'm very pleased . . . extremely! Please sit down! Only don't sit on the sofa, the back leg is broken. Do sit down, Senya!'

. We sat down. . . . There was a silence, during which Pupkin stroked his knee, while I felt embarrassed and tried not to look at my wife.

'Mm, yes . . .' my uncle began, lighting a cigar (he always smokes cigars when he has guests). 'So you're married now. . . . That's how it is. . . . It's a good thing in a way. . . . You have your dear one with you, love, romance; on the other hand, there's children—as soon as they start to appear you'll be howling your head off! Boots for one, trousers for another, school bills for the third. . . . Good God Almighty! Thank God, my wife produced dead ones— half of them!'

'How have you been keeping?' I asked, hoping to change the subject.

'Badly, my boy! The other day I was prostrate all day. . . . My chest bursting, shivering fits, temperature. . . . My wife says: "Take quinine and don't lose your temper. . . ."

But how can I help losing my temper? Only this morning I ordered the snow to be cleared from the porch a bit, and d'you think anyone's done anything? None of these beggars would lift his little finger. . . . I couldn't clean it myself, could I? I'm ailing, weak. . . . I've got concealed piles.'

I was embarrassed and blew my nose loudly.

'Or perhaps I got it from the baths . . .' my uncle went on, looking thoughtfully out of the window. 'Perhaps! You know, I went to the baths on Thursday. . . . I steamed myself for about three hours. But the steam makes the piles break out all the more. The doctors say that baths aren't good for the health. . . . That's wrong, madam. . . . I've been used to them from childhood because my father kept baths in Kiev, in the Kreshchatik. . . . Sometimes I used to steam myself all day long. . . . Particularly as I didn't have to pay. . . .'

I could not bear the shame of it any longer. I stood up and began to stammer out my good-byes.

'Why, where are you off to?' said my uncle, surprised, and he seized me by the sleeve. 'Your auntie's just coming! Let's have a bite of what's going, we'll have some liqueur! . . . There's some salted beef, Mitya's run off to fetch some sausage. . . . How you do stand on ceremony, really! Snooty, Senya, that's what you are. That's bad, that is! You didn't order the wedding-dress from Gasha! You know, madam, my daughter has a dressmaking business. . . . I know Madame Stepanid made your dress, but Stepanidka can't touch us. And what's more, we'd have done it cheaper. . . .'

I cannot remember how I took leave of my uncle, how I reached the carriage. . . . I felt that I was crushed, humiliated, and every minute I expected to hear the contemptuous laugh of my well-educated wife. . . .

God, what vulgarity we're in for at Plevkov's! I thought, going cold with horror. If only we can get it over as quickly as possible, to hell with them all! And what a misfortune—I

don't know a single general! I do know one retired colonel,
and he keeps a pub! Oh, I really have no luck! 'Sonechka,'
I said to my wife in a tearful voice. 'Forgive me for taking you
to that pig-sty just now. . . . I thought I'd give you
something to laugh about, that you'd have a chance to
observe some odd types. . . . It's not my fault that it
turned out to be so vulgar, so disgusting. . . . I'm
sorry. . . .'

I looked shyly at my wife, and saw that my worst fears
were confirmed. My wife's eyes were full of tears, a blush
either of shame or anger burned on her cheeks, her hands
convulsively plucked at the fringe of the carriage window.
. . . I was thrown into a fever and shuddered from fear. . . .

Well, this is where my ignominy begins! I thought, feeling
my hands and feet turning to lead. 'But I'm really not to
blame, Sonya!'—a wail broke from me. 'How silly of you,
really! Of course they're pigs, vulgar, but after all it wasn't
me who made them my relations!'

'If you don't like your common relations,' Sonya sobbed,
looking at me with imploring eyes, 'then you certainly
won't like mine. . . . I'm ashamed, and I can't bring
myself to make a clean breast of it. . . . Darling, my sweet.
. . . In a moment Baroness Scheppling will start telling
you how Mummy worked as her housekeeper, and how
ungrateful Mummy and I are for not showing our gratitude
for her past kindness to us now that she has fallen on hard
times. . . . But please don't believe her! The old tartar's
a liar. . . . I swear to you that we send her a sugar-loaf
and a pound of tea on every holiday! . . .'

'But you're not serious, Sonya, are you?' I said in amazement, and felt the lead leaving my limbs and my whole body
regaining its bouyancy. 'You give sugar and a pound of tea
to the baroness! . . . Gosh!'

'And when you meet General Jerebchikov's wife, don't
laugh at her, darling. She's so unfortunate! If she cries all
the time and talks nonsense, it's because Count Derzai-

Chertovchinov has robbed her. She'll complain about her fate and will ask you for a loan; but you—don't give her anything. . . . It would be all right if she were to spend it on herself, but she'll just give it to the Count.'

'Sweetie . . . angel!' And I set about embracing my wife from sheer delight. 'My ducky-wucky! This really is a surprise! If you were to tell me that your Baroness Scheppling (with two "p's") walks about the streets stark naked you'd have done me an even greater favour! Give me your little hand!'

And suddenly I was sorry that I had refused my uncle's salted beef, that I had not strummed on his paralytic piano, had not drunk his liqueur. . . . But then I remembered that at Plevkov's they served good brandy, and sucking-pig with horse-radish.

'Off to Plevkov's!' I shouted to the driver at the top of my voice.

TÆDIUM VITÆ

It has been observed by experienced
people that neither do *recluses* part
with this life easily; besides, they
often reveal what is so typical for
people of their age—avarice and
greed, as well as mistrustfulness,
pusillanimity, stubborness, dis-
content, etc.

(*Practical Manual for Priests* by
P. Nechayev.)

ANNA MIKHAILOVNA LEBEDEV, a colonel's wife, lost her
only daughter, a young girl who was engaged to be married.
This death brought with it another death: the old woman,
stunned by God's visitation, felt that all her past had
irrevocably died and that now a new life was beginning for
her—a life which had very little in common with the first
one. . . .

She bustled about aimlessly, without any system. To begin
with, she sent one thousand roubles to a Mount Athos
monastery and donated half the household silver to the
cemetery church. After a little while she gave up smoking,
and made a vow not to eat meat. But none of this made her
feel any better—on the contrary, the feeling of old age and
the nearness of death became all the sharper and more
emphatic. Then Anna Mikhailovna sold her town house for
a mere song, and hurried away to her country house without
any definite aim in view.

As soon as someone consciously begins to question the
point of existence—in no matter what way—and feels an
acute need to look beyond the grave, then neither sacrifices,
nor fasting, nor knocking about from place to place will
satisfy him. But, fortunately for Anna Mikhailovna, just as

she arrived at Jenino, fate brought her face to face with an occurrence which made her forget about old age and the nearness of death for a long time. It so happened that on the day of her arrival Martyn, the cook, spilt boiling water on both his feet. Someone galloped off to fetch the local doctor, but he was not at home. Then Anna Mikhailovna, who was fastidious and sensitive, washed Martyn's wounds with her own hands, put ointment on them, and bandaged both feet. She sat up all night by the cook's bedside. When, thanks to her efforts, Martyn ceased to groan and fell asleep, something—as she later recounted—'dawned' in her heart. It suddenly seemed to her that her aim in life was revealed, and was as clear as daylight. . . . Pale, with swimming eyes, she reverently kissed Martyn's forehead as he slept, and began to pray.

After that Madame Lebedev took up medical work. In the days of her sinful, slipshod life—which she now remembered only with abhorrence—she had undergone a good deal of medical treatment herself because she had had nothing else to do.

Besides, doctors had been numbered among her lovers, and she had learned a bit from them. Both these facts stood her in good stead now. She ordered a medicine chest, some books, and a journal called *The Doctor*, and bravely set about giving people medical treatment. At first only the inhabitants of Jenino came to her for treatment, but later on people started to flock to her from all the villages around.

'Just imagine, my dear!' she boasted to the priest's wife about three months after her arrival. 'Yesterday I had sixteen patients, and today I had a whole twenty of them! They tired me out so much that I can scarcely stand on my feet. Do you know, I've run out of laudanum! There's an epidemic of dysentery in Gourino.'

Every morning when she woke up she remembered that there were patients waiting for her, and her heart gave an agreeable shiver. When she had dressed and hurriedly drunk her tea, she would begin to receive patients. The procedure of receiving them gave her inexpressible delight. First, as if wishing to prolong this delight, she would slowly enter the patients' names in an exercise book, and then she would call each one in turn. The greater the suffering of the patient and the dirtier and more disgusting his ailment, the sweeter her work seemed to her. Nothing gave her so much pleasure as the thought that she was struggling against her fastidiousness and not sparing herself, and she purposely tried to take more time in rummaging in suppurating wounds. There were moments when, as if enraptured by the hideousness and stench of a wound, she would fall into a sort of ecstatic cynicism when she felt an uncontrollable desire to force her nature—and in these moments it seemed to her that she was at the summit of her vocation. She adored her patients. Sentiment suggested that they were her saviours, but reason made her want to see them not as individual personalities, not as peasants, but as something abstract—the people! That is why she was unusually soft and timid with them, blushed in front of them for her mistakes and, while she was receiving them, always had a guilty appearance. . . .

After each reception of patients, which took up more than half a day, weary, red from strain, and sick, she would hasten to pass the time by reading. She used to read medical books, or those Russian authors who most closely accorded with her mood.

Having thus begun a new life, Anna Mikhailovna felt fresh, satisfied, and almost happy. She did not even desire a fuller life. And then, just as if to crown her happiness, a kind of dessert after a good meal, it so turned out that she became reconciled with her husband, towards whom she had a deep feeling of guilt. Seventeen years before, shortly after the birth of her daughter, she had been unfaithful to her husband, Arkadiy Petrovich, and they had had to separate. She had not seen him since then. He was serving somewhere in the south in the artillery as battery commander, and now and

again—about twice a year—he used to send his daughter
letters, which she would carefully hide from her mother.
Then, after their daughter's death, Anna Mikhailovna
unexpectedly received a long letter from him. In elderly,
feeble handwriting he wrote to her that, with the death of
his only daughter, he had lost the last thing that bound him
to life, that he was old, ill, and longing for death of which,
at the same time, he was afraid. He complained that he was
fed up with everything, sick of everything, that he no longer
got on well with people, and that he could hardly wait for
the time when he would hand over the battery and get as
far away as possible from petty gossip. In conclusion, he
asked his wife for God's sake to pray for him, to take care of
herself, and not to give way to despondency. An assiduous
correspondence between the old people ensued. So far as it
was possible to judge from subsequent letters—which were
all equally tearful and gloomy—the colonel was not only
distressed by disease and the loss of his daughter: he had run
into debt, quarrelled with his superiors and with his brother
officers, neglected his battery to such an extent that it was
impossible to hand it over, and so on. This correspondence
between husband and wife went on for about two years, and
ended up with the old man retiring and coming to live at
Jenino.

He arrived one February afternoon, when the buildings
of Jenino were hidden by deep snowdrifts, and in the clear,
blue air, in addition to the sharp, hard frost, there was a
death-like silence.

Watching him from the window as he got out of the sleigh,
Anna Mikhailovna did not recognise her husband. He was a
small, bent old man, who was now quite decrepit and
unbalanced. What struck Anna Mikhailovna first were the
elderly folds on his long neck, and his thin legs with stiffly
bending knees, like artificial legs. As he paid the driver he
made a long statement to him about something or other, and
finally spat angrily.

'It disgusts me even to talk to you!' Anna Mikhailovna overheard his elderly grumbling. 'You should realise that it's immoral to ask for a tip! Everyone should only get what he's earned—that's how it is!'

When he came into the hall Anna Mikhailovna saw a yellow face—which even the frost had not coloured—with protuberant prawn-like eyes, and a scanty beard in which grey hairs were mixed with red ones. Arkadiy Petrovich embraced his wife with one arm and kissed her on the forehead. As they looked at each other the old people somehow felt afraid of something and were terribly embarrassed, just as if they were ashamed of their old age.

'You're just in time!' Anna Mikhailovna hastened to say. 'Dinner is just ready. You must be hungry after your journey!'

They sat down to dinner. The first course was eaten in silence. Arkadiy Petrovich took a fat notebook out of his pocket and looked at some notes, while his wife studiously prepared the salad. They both of them had plenty of material for conversation, but neither of them drew on it. They both felt that memories of their daughter would cause acute pain and tears, while from the past, as from a deep, vinegary barrel, wafted stuffiness and murk. . . .

'But you're not eating any meat!' remarked Arkadiy Petrovich.

'No, I made a vow not to eat any . . .' his wife answered quietly.

'Why? It isn't bad for your health. . . . If you analyse it chemically, then fish and all lenten fare is made up of the same elements as meat. In actual fact, there's no such thing as lenten fare. . . .' (Why am I saying this? thought the old man.) 'For example, this cucumber is no more lenten fare than chicken. . . .'

'Oh, yes it is. When I eat a cucumber, then I know that they didn't deprive it of life, that blood wasn't shed. . . .'

'That, my dear, is an optical illusion. You eat a great

deal of infusoria with a cucumber—and wasn't the cucumber itself alive? Plants are organisms too! And what about fish?'

What am I talking this nonsense for? thought Arkadiy Petrovich again, and quickly began to talk about the advances being made in chemistry.

'It's really a miracle!' he said, chewing his bread with difficulty. 'They'll soon be making milk chemically, and I dare say they'll get as far as making meat! Yes! In a thousand years time instead of a kitchen there'll be a chemical laboratory in every house where, from gases and so forth that don't cost anything, they'll make everything you want!'

Anna Mikhailovna looked at his uneasily restless, prawn-like eyes, and listened. She felt that the old man was talking about chemistry only so as not to talk about anything else, but nevertheless his theory about lenten and non-lenten fare interested her.

'You retired as a general?' she asked, when he suddenly fell silent and began blowing his nose.

'Yes, as a general. . . . "Your Excellency". . . .'

The general talked all through dinner without stopping, thus displaying his inordinate garrulity—a characteristic which, long ago in their youth, Anna Mikhailovna had not noticed in him. The old woman's head began to ache from his chattering.

After dinner he went to his room for a rest, but though tired, he did not succeed in falling asleep. When, before the evening tea, the old woman went in to him, he was lying hunched up under the blanket, goggling at the ceiling, and emitting occasional sighs.

'What's the matter with you, Arkadiy?' said Anna Mikhailovna in horror, looking at his grey and drawn face.

'N-nothing . . .' he said. 'Rheumatism.'

'Why didn't you say so? I might be able to help you!'

'You can't help. . . .'

'If it's rheumatism, then you should paint yourself with iodine and take sodium salicylate internally. . . .'

'That's all rubbish. . . . I've been having treatment for eight years. . . . Don't stamp your feet like that!' the general suddenly shouted at the old maid-servant, angrily opening his eyes wide as he looked at her. 'She's stamping like a horse!'

Anna Mikhailovna and the maid, who had long ago become unaccustomed to such a tone of voice, looked at each other and blushed. Noticing their confusion, the general frowned and turned towards the wall.

'I must warn you, Anyuta . . .' he groaned, 'I've got an insufferable temper! I've become irritable in my old age. . . .'

'You should try to overcome it . . .' sighed Anna Mikhailovna.

'It's easy enough to say "you should"! And I shouldn't have any pain, either, but then Nature doesn't pay any heed to our "shoulds". Ow! But you go away, Anyuta. . . . When the pains come on I find the presence of people trying. . . . It's difficult to talk. . . .'

Days, weeks, months elapsed, and little by little Arkadiy Petrovich began to feel at home in his new place: he became used to it, and people became used to him. At first he lived in the house without ever going out, but his old age and the burden of his intolerable temper were felt throughout Jenino. He usually woke up very early, at about four o'clock in the morning; his day started with a shrill, elderly cough which woke up Anna Mikhailovna and all the servants. So as somehow to kill the long time from early morning till dinner, if his legs were not fettered by rheumatism he would wander through all the rooms and carp at the untidiness which he thought he saw everywhere. Everything annoyed him: the laziness of the servants, loud footsteps, cocks crowing, smoke from the kitchen, church bells. . . . He grumbled, swore, harried the servants—but after every swear word he would clutch his head and say in a tearful voice:

'God, what a temper I've got! An insufferable temper!'

But at dinner he would eat a great deal and chatter incessantly. He talked about socialism, about new military reforms, about hygiene, and Anna Mikhailovna would listen to him and feel that he was saying all this only so as not to talk about their daughter and about the past. In each other's presence they still felt awkward and as if they were ashamed of something. It was only in the evenings, when darkness filled the rooms and a cricket chirped despondently behind the stove, that this awkwardness disappeared. They sat side by side in silence, and on those occasions it was just as if their souls were whispering about the thing that neither of them could bring themselves to say aloud. On those occasions, warming each other with the remains of life's fire, each of them understood perfectly what the other was thinking about. But no sooner did the maid bring in the lamp than the old man would again fall to chattering or grumbling about the untidiness. He had absolutely nothing to do. Anna Mikhailovna had wanted to draw him into her medical work, but at the very first reception of patients he had yawned and looked bored. Nor did she succeed in making him interested in reading. Used as he had been to reading at odd moments when he was in the army, he did not know how to read for a long time, for hours at a stretch. It was enough for him to read five or six short pages to become tired and take his glasses off.

But spring came, and the general abruptly changed his way of life. When newly-trodden paths ran from the garden to the green field and the village, and birds began to stir in the trees in front of the window, quite unexpectedly for Anna Mikhailovna, he took to going to church. He went to church not only on feast days, but on weekdays too. This religious zeal started with the Mass which the old man had ordered for his daughter, without telling his wife. He knelt throughout the Mass, bowed himself to the ground, wept and, it seemed to him, prayed fervently. But it was not a prayer that he said. Giving himself up to his fatherly feeling and

calling up his beloved daughter's face in his memory, he
looked at the ikons and whispered:

'Shurochka! My darling child! My angel!'

It was a paroxysm of elderly grief, but the old man
imagined that a reaction, a radical change was taking place
in him. Next day he again felt drawn to go to church, on the
day after too. . . . He used to come back from church fresh,
radiant, with a smile all over his face. During dinner religion
and theological questions began to serve him as a theme for
his incessant chatter. On entering his room Anna Mikhailovna several times caught him turning over the pages of the
Gospels. But unfortunately this religious fervour did not last
long. After one particularly sharp attack of rheumatism,
which lasted for a whole week, he stopped going to church:
he somehow did not remember that he had to go to Mass. . . .

He suddenly felt a desire for company.

'I can't understand how one can live like that, without
seeing anyone!' he began to grumble. 'I must go and pay
calls on the neighbours. It may be stupid, futile, but while
I'm alive I must submit to the laws of society!'

Anna Mikhailovna offered him the horses. He paid calls
on the neighbours, but did not go to see them a second time.
The necessity for seeing people was satisfied by him trotting
about the village and finding fault with the peasants.

One morning he was sitting in the dining-room before an
open window and drinking tea. In the little front garden
outside the window the peasants who had come to Anna
Mikhailovna for treatment were sitting on benches beside the
lilac and gooseberry bushes. The old man screwed his eyes
up at them for a long time, then grumbled:

'Ces moujiks! . . . Objects of civic sorrow. . . . Rather
than trying to cure your illnesses, you'd do better to go and
get treated for all your moral filth and rottenness.'

Anna Mikhailovna, who adored her patients, stopped
pouring out the tea and looked at the old man in dumb
amazement. The patients, who had never met with anything

but kindness and warm sympathy in the Lebedev house, were also astonished, and got up from their seats.

'Yes, my dear sirs. . . . ces moujiks . . .' the general went on. 'You surprise me. You surprise me very much! Well, aren't they animals?' the old man turned to Anna Mikhailovna. 'The local authorities gave them an advance so that they could sow oats, and they just went and drank their oats away! It wasn't only one or two of them who spent it all on drink, but all of them! The pub-keepers didn't have enough storeroom for all the oats. . . . Was that right?' the general turned to the peasants, 'Eh? Was it?'

'Don't, Arkadiy!' whispered Anna Mikhailovna.

'Do you think the local authorities got those oats for nothing? What sort of citizens are you after that, if you don't respect either your own property, or anyone else's, or public property? You drank away those oats . . . you cut down the wood, and drank that away too. You steal everything. . . . My wife gives you treatment, and you went and stole her fence. . . . Was that right?'

'That's enough!' groaned the general's wife.

'It's time you pulled yourselves together . . .' Lebedev went on grumbling. 'You are a disgrace to look at! You there, with the red hair, you came for treatment—your feet hurt?—but you didn't bother to wash your feet at home. . . . The dirt's an inch thick! You boor, you hope it'll be washed here? They got it into their heads that they . . . ces moujiks . . . just imagine that they can ride rough-shod over people. The priest married a certain Fyodor, the local carpenter. The carpenter didn't pay him a penny. "Too poor!" he says. "I can't!" Well, all right. Only the priest ordered a little bookshelf from Fyodor. . . . And what d'you think? He went five or six times to the priest to collect his money! Eh? Well, wasn't he a swine? He didn't pay the priest himself, but. . . .'

'The priest's got plenty of money without that . . .' boomed one of the patients sullenly.

'And how do you know?' the general burst out, jumping up and hanging out of the window. 'Have you looked in the priest's pocket? And even if he were a millionaire, you shouldn't take advantage of his work without paying! You don't work for nothing yourself, so don't take something for nothing. You can't imagine how disgusting they are!' the general turned to Anna Mikhailovna. 'You should have seen some of them in court, or at their meetings! They're brigands!'

The general did not even calm down when the reception of patients began. He nagged and mimicked every patient, and explained all their illnesses as the result of drunkenness and debauch.

'Look how thin you are!' he prodded one man in the ribs with his finger. 'And why? Nothing to eat! You've drunk it all away. Didn't you drink away all the local authorities' oats?'

'There are no two ways about it,' sighed the sick man, 'we lived better as serfs. . . .'

'Rot! You're lying!' the general exploded. 'Why, you're not sincere about it, you're only saying it to flatter!'

Next day the general once more sat at the window and told off the peasants. This occupation fascinated him, and he took to sitting by the window every day. When Anna Mikhailovna saw that her husband was not calming down, she began to receive her patients in the barn, but the general found his way to the barn as well. The old woman bore this 'trial' submissively, and only expressed a protest by blushing and distributing money to the patients who had been sworn at; but when the patients, who had taken a strong dislike to the general, began coming to her more and more rarely, she could not contain herself. One day at dinner, when the general made some sort of joke about the patients, her eyes became bloodshot and her face twitched.

'I'd beg you to leave my patients in peace . . .' she said, sternly. 'If you feel a need to vent your temper on someone,

then you can give me a dressing-down, but leave them alone.
. . . Thanks to you, they've stopped coming for treatment.'

'Aha! They've stopped coming!' the general smirked.
'They're offended! By Jove, if someone's angry it means he's
in the wrong. Ha, ha. . . . But it's a good thing, Anyuta,
that they've stopped coming. I'm very glad. . . . Why,
your treatment doesn't do anything but harm! Instead of
going to be treated scientifically by a doctor at the rural
hospital, they go to you to be treated with soda and castor
oil whatever illness they may have. It does great harm!'

Anna Mikhailovna looked at the old man intently,
thought a minute, and suddenly went pale.

'Of course,' the general went on jabbering. 'In medicine
knowledge is necessary above all, but philanthropy without
any knowledge is quackery. And what's more, according to
the law you haven't the right to treat people. In my opinion,
you'll do much more good to a sick man if you shove him off
roughly to see the doctor, than if you treat him yourself.'

The general was silent for a moment, and then continued:

'If you don't like the way I talk to them well, then I won't
speak to them any more although, as a matter of fact . . .
in all conscience it's much better to be frank with them than
to keep silent and worship them. Alexander of Macedon was
a great man, but there's no need to go and make a song and
dance about it, and it's the same with the Russian people—
it's a great people, but it doesn't follow that you can't tell
it the truth to its face. You can't make a lap-dog of the
people. These ces moujiks are human-beings just like you
and me, with the same shortcomings, and therefore you
shouldn't worship them, nor coddle them, but you should
teach them, reform them . . . inspire them. . . .'

'It's not for us to teach them . . .' the general's wife
muttered. 'We can learn something from them.'

'What can we learn?'

'Lots of things. For instance . . . how to work hard. . . .'

'How to work hard? Eh? You said: "How to work hard?"'

12

The general choked, jumped up from the table, and began to pace the room.

'And I haven't worked hard?' he burst out. 'And anyway. . . . I'm an intellectual, and not a moujik, why should I work hard? I. . . . I'm an intellectual!'

The old man was really offended, and his face bore a boyishly peeved expression.

'Thousands of soldiers passed through my hands. . . . I rotted away in the war, caught rheumatism for the rest of my life and . . . and I didn't work hard! Perhaps you'll tell me, I can learn how to suffer from that people of yours? Of course, it isn't as if I'd ever suffered? I lost my own daughter . . . the only thing that still tied me to life in this damned old age! And I haven't suffered!'

At this sudden memory of their daughter the old people all at once began to weep and to wipe their eyes with their table-napkins.

'And we aren't suffering!' whimpered the general, giving himself up to his tears. 'They have an aim in life . . . faith, whereas we have nothing but problems . . . problems and horror! We don't suffer!'

The old people both felt sorry for each other. They sat side by side, sympathised with each other, and wept together for two hours. After this they could at last look each other openly in the face, and boldly talk about their daughter, about the past, and about the threatening future.

That evening they both went to bed in the same room. The old man talked incessantly, and prevented his wife from sleeping.

'God, what a temper I've got!' he said. 'Now why did I say all that to you? Why, those were illusions, and it's natural for man to live on illusions, especially in old age. With my jabbering I took your last consolation away from you. You would have gone on treating the peasants till your dying day and eating no meat, but no—the devil prompted me. It's impossible without illusions. . . . Sometimes whole

states live on illusions. . . . Famous writers are clever
if anyone is, but they can't get along without illusions
either. Why, that favourite of yours wrote seven volumes on
"the people"!'

An hour later the general turned over and said:

'And why is it precisely in old age that people pay
attention to their feelings and criticise their actions? Why
don't they pay any attention to it in youth? Old age is
unbearable anyway, without that. . . . Yes. . . . In youth
the whole of life passes without leaving a trace, scarcely
making any impression on consciousness, whereas in old age
the slightest feeling is firmly fixed in one's head and raises
a heap of problems. . . .'

The old people fell asleep late, but got up early. In
general, after Anna Mikhailovna gave up her medical work,
they slept little and badly, and as a result life seemed twice
as long to them. . . . They shortened their nights with
conversation, and spent their days loafing about the rooms
or the garden, and casting questioning glances into each
other's eyes.

Towards the end of the summer fate sent the old people
one more 'illusion'. Once, when Anna Mikhailovna went
into her husband's room, she found him engrossed in an
interesting occupation: he was sitting at the table and greedily
eating grated radish and hemp oil. The muscles of his face
were working, and saliva was dripping round the corners of
his mouth.

'Have some, Anyuta!' he offered. 'It's splendid!'

Anna Mikhailovna tried the radish with some hesitation,
and began to eat. Soon an expression of greed appeared on
her face too. . . .

'It would be nice to have some of that . . . what d'you
call it?' the general said that evening as he was going to bed.
'It would be nice the way the Jews do it, rip open a pike's
belly, take out the roe, fresh, you know, and some spring
onions. . . .'

'Well, why not? It's not difficult to catch a pike!'

The general, undressed as he was and barefoot, went off to the kitchen, woke up the cook, and ordered him to catch a pike. In the morning Anna Mikhailovna suddenly felt like having some smoked sturgeon, and Martyn had to gallop off to town for it.

'Oh!' the old woman said in alarm, 'I forgot to tell him to get some peppermint cakes while he is about it! I'd like to have something sweet. . . .'

The old people gave themselves up to gustatory sensations. They never left the kitchen, and competed with each other at thinking up new dishes. The general wracked his brains, remembered his bachelor camp life, when he had had some culinary experience himself, and invented. . . . Among the dishes they invented they especially liked one, prepared from rice, grated cheese, eggs, and the gravy from overdone meat. This dish requires a great deal of pepper and bay-leaves.

The last 'illusion' ended with this spicy dish. It fell to its lot to be the last delight of both lives.

'It looks like rain . . .' said the general, who was working up for a stroke, one September night. 'I don't think I should have eaten so much of that rice to-day. . . . I feel very heavy.'

The general's wife was spread out on the bed, breathing heavily. She felt stifled. . . . She, like the old man, had a stomach ache.

'And what's more, my legs are itching, damn them . . .' grumbled the old man. 'I've got some sort of itch from the soles of my feet to my knees. . . . It hurts and it itches . . . it's unbearable, damn it! But I'm keeping you awake. . . . I'm sorry. . . .'

More than an hour passed in silence. Little by little Anna Mikhailovna became used to the heaviness in her stomach, and dozed off. The old man sat up in bed, put his head on his knees, and sat like that for a long time. Then he began to scratch his shins. The more assiduously his nails worked, the worse the itch became.

After a little while the wretched old man climbed off the bed and hobbled about the room. He looked out of the window. . . . There, outside the window, in bright moonlight, the cold of autumn was gradually shackling dying nature. He could see the cold, grey fog shrouding the withering grass, and the freezing wood awake and shuddering with what remained of its yellow leaves.

The general sat down on the floor, grasped his knees, and put his head on them.

'Anyuta!' he called.

The old woman, who was a light sleeper, turned over and opened her eyes.

'You know what I was thinking, Anyuta?' the old man began. 'You're not asleep? I was thinking that the most natural interest in old age should be children. . . . What do you think? But if there aren't any children, then people have to take an interest in something else. . . . It would be a good thing to be a writer . . . or an artist . . . or a scholar . . . when one's old. . . . They say that when Gladstone has nothing to do he studies the ancient classics and—it absorbs him. So that if he is thrown out of office, he'll have something to fill up his life. And in the same way it would be a good thing to go in for mysticism . . . or . . . or. . . .'

The old man scratched his legs and went on:

'But it also happens that old people fall into second childhood—you know, when they want to plant trees, wear medals . . . take up spiritualism. . . .'

A light snore came from the old woman. The general stood up and again looked out of the window. The cold morosely asked to be let in, and the fog had already crept up to the wood and was shrouding the tree trunks.

How many more months to spring? thought the old man, pressing his forehead against the cold glass. October . . . November . . . December . . . six months!

And these six months somehow appeared to him as something endlessly long, as long as his old age. He limped round the room and sat down on the bed.

'Anyuta!' he called.

'Well?'

'Is your medicine chest locked?'

'No, why?'

'Nothing. I want to put some iodine on my legs.'

Silence ensued once more.

'Anyuta!' The old man woke up his wife.

'What?'

'Are the bottles labelled?'

'Yes, yes.'

The general slowly lit a candle, and went out of the room.

For a long time the sleepy Anna Mikhailovna could hear his bare feet dragging and the tinkling of medicine bottles. Finally he came back, groaned, and lay down.

He did not wake up in the morning. Whether he just died, or whether it was because he had been to the medicine chest, Anna Mikhailovna did not know. And anyway, she was too shaken to inquire into the causes of his death. . . .

Once more she began to bustle about aimlessly, nervously, without any system. Donations, fasts, vows, collections for pilgrimages began again. . . .

'I want to go to a convent!' she whispered, pressing herself in fear to the old maid-servant. 'To a convent!'

OTHER PEOPLE'S TROUBLE

❊

IT was hardly six o'clock in the morning when Kovalyov, a newly-fledged lawyer, got into the carriage with his young wife and drove off along a country lane. He and his wife had never got up early before, and now the splendour of the quiet summer morning seemed to them like something out of a fairy tale. The earth, clad in green and besprinkled with diamonds of dew, looked beautiful and happy. Sun-rays were falling in bright patches on the wood, were quivering in the sparkling river, and in the unusually clear blue air there was such freshness that it seemed as if the whole of God's world had just had a bath, and become younger and healthier in consequence.

For the Kovalyovs—as they themselves acknowledged later —this was the happiest morning of their honeymoon, and therefore of their whole lives. They chattered without stopping, sang, roared with laughter for no reason, and played the fool to such an extent that finally they felt ashamed of behaving like that in front of the coachman. Not only in the present, but in the future, too, it seemed that happiness would be theirs: they were going to buy an estate —a little 'romantic spot' of which they had been dreaming since the day they were married. The future held the most brilliant expectations for them both. He dreamed of his future work in rural self government, of rational methods of agriculture, of the work of his own hands and other blessings about which he had read and heard so much, while she was attracted by the purely romantic side of the business: shady avenues, fishing, fragrant nights. . . .

What with laughter and conversation they did not notice

that they had driven twelve miles. Court-Councillor Mikhailov's estate, which they were going to look at, stood on a
high and steep river bank, and was hidden behind a birch-
grove. . . . The red roof was hardly visible because of the
thick green, and all the clay bank was planted with young
saplings.

'The view's not bad!' said Kovalyov, as the carriage drove
through a ford to the other side of the river. 'The house is
on the hill, and at the foot of the hill there's a river! It's
damn attractive! Only, you know, Verochka, those steps
don't fit in at all . . . they spoil the whole view, they're so
clumsy. . . . If we buy this estate then we must certainly
put some wrought-iron steps. . . .'

Verochka liked the view too. Laughing loudly, and with
affectation in every limb, she ran up the steps with her
husband after her, and both of them, dishevelled and out of
breath, went into the coppice. The first person to meet them
near the house was a big peasant, sleepy, hairy, and morose.
He was sitting by a little porch and cleaning a child's boot.

'Is Mr. Mikhailov at home?' Kovalyov asked him. 'Go
and tell him that some prospective buyers have come to see
the estate.'

The peasant looked at the Kovalyovs with dumb amazement and ambled off slowly—not to the house, but to the
kitchen, which was at the side of the house. At the same
instant faces—each one sleepier and more astonished than
the last—flashed for a moment at the kitchen window.

'Prospective buyers have arrived!' a whisper could be
heard. 'Good heavens! Mikhalkovo is being sold! Look, how
young they are!'

Somewhere a dog barked, and an angry wail could be
heard, such as cats give when their tails are stepped on.
The servants' agitation was soon also communicated to the
chickens, geese and turkeys which were peacefully pacing
up and down the paths. Soon a lad who looked like a servant
darted out of the kitchen; he peered at the Kovalyovs and

ran to the house, putting his coat on as he went. . . . The Kovalyovs thought this commotion very funny, and they could hardly contain their laughter.

'What funny faces!' said Kovalyov, exchanging a glance with his wife. 'They look at us as if we were savages!'

At last a little man with a clean-shaven, elderly face and dishevelled hair came out of the house. . . . He clicked his heels—he was wearing ragged slippers embroidered with gold—smiled sourly, and fixed a stony stare on his unbidden guests. . . .

'Mr. Mikhailov?' Kovalyov began, raising his hat.' How do you do? . . . My wife here and I read the Land Bank's advertisement about the sale of your estate, and now we have come to have a look at it. . . . We may buy it. . . . Would you be kind enough to show it us? . . .'

Mikhailov gave another sour smile, became embarrassed, and blinked his eyes. In his confusion he made his hair even more dishevelled, and such a comical expression of shame and bewilderment appeared on his clean-shaven face that Kovalyov and his Verochka looked at each other and could not refrain from smiling.

'Very pleased to meet you, sir,' he mumbled. 'At your service. . . . Have you come a long way, sir?'

'From Konkov. . . . We're living in a villa there.'

'In a villa. . . . Are you? . . . Extraordinary business! Welcome! You must forgive us, but we've only just got up, and it's not very tidy.'

Smiling sourly and rubbing his hands, Mikhailov led his guests to the other side of the house. Kovalyov put on his glasses and, with the look of an expert tourist surveying the sights, began to inspect the estate. He saw first a big stone house of old-fashioned, heavy design, and covered with coats-of-arms, lions and peeling stucco. The roof had not been painted for a long time, the windows had iridescent glass, grass was growing in the chinks between the steps. Everything was dilapidated and neglected, but on the whole they liked the house. It looked romantic, modest and benign, like an old maiden aunt. In front of it, a few paces from the front door, shone a pond, on which floated two ducks and a toy boat. Birch trees, all of the same height and thickness, grew round the pond.

'Aha! And there's a pond too!' said Kovalyov, screwing up his eyes against the sun. 'That's very attractive. Are there any crucians in it?'

'Yes, sir. . . . There used to be carp in it too once, but then when they stopped cleaning the pond, the carp all died.'

'A pity,' said Kovalyov in the tone of a mentor. 'A pond should be cleaned as often as possible—all the more so as slime and waterweeds make splendid fertiliser for the fields. You know what, Vera? When we buy this estate, let's build a summerhouse on piles in the middle of the pond, with a little bridge leading to it. I saw a summerhouse like that at Prince Afrontov's.'

'We could have tea in the summerhouse . . .' Verochka sighed sweetly.

'Yes. . . . But what's that tower there with a steeple?'

'That's the visitors' annexe,' Mikhailov answered.

'How out of place it is, sticking up there! We'll pull it down. In general, a great deal will have to be pulled down. A very great deal!'

Suddenly they heard, clearly and distinctly, the sound of a woman weeping. The Kovalyovs looked round at the house, but at the same time one of the windows banged, and through the opalescent glass two big eyes, wet with tears, flashed only for a moment. The person who was weeping was obviously ashamed of her tears and, slamming the window, had hidden behind the curtain.

'Wouldn't you like to look at the garden and the out-houses?' said Mikhailov quickly, wrinkling his face—wrinkled enough as it was—into a sour smile. 'Come along . . . after all, the most important thing is not the house but . . . but the rest. . . .'

The Kovalyovs went off to look at the stables and barns.
The lawyer made the round of each barn, looked about,
sniffed everything, and showed off his knowledge of agriculture. He inquired how many acres the estate had and how
many head of cattle, criticised Russia for cutting down her
forests, reproached Mikhailov for letting so much manure
be wasted, and so on. As he was talking he kept on glancing
at his Verochka, who did not take her loving eyes off him for
a moment and thought: How clever he is!

While they were inspecting the cattle-sheds they once
more heard someone crying.

'Listen, who is that crying there?' asked Verochka.

Mikhailov made a gesture with his hand and turned away.

'Odd,' murmured Verochka, when the whimpering
changed to interminable hysterical weeping. 'It's just as if
someone was being beaten or slaughtered.'

'It's my wife, don't take any notice of her . . .' said
Mikhailov.

'Why on earth is she crying?'

'She's a weak woman, madam! She can't bear to see her
family home being sold.'

'Well, why are you selling it?' asked Verochka.

'We're not selling it, madam, it's the bank. . . .'

'That's strange, why do you let them?'

Mikhailov glanced in amazement at Verochka's pink face
and shrugged his shoulders.

'We have to pay the interest,' he said. 'Two thousand
one hundred roubles every year! And where can we get it
from? It's enough to make anyone howl. Women are weak,
of course. There she is, sorry about her family home, sorry
for the children and for me . . . and ashamed in front of
the servants. . . . When you said just now, over there by
the pond, that this would have to be pulled down and that
would have to be built, it was just like a knife in her heart.'

When they went back past the house the Kovalyovs saw a
school-boy with close-cropped hair and two little girls—

Mikhailov's children—at the windows. What were the children thinking, as they looked at the prospective buyers? Verochka probably understood their thoughts. . . . When she took her seat in the carriage to drive home the fresh morning and her dreams of a 'romantic spot' no longer had any charm for her.

'How unpleasant it all is!' she said to her husband. 'Really, we should give them two thousand one hundred roubles! Let them go on living on their estate. . . .'

'You're a clever one, aren't you!' laughed Kovalyov. 'Of course, one's sorry for them, but after all they have themselves to blame. Why did they mortgage the estate? Why have they neglected it so? One shouldn't even waste any pity on them. If that estate were intelligently developed, if one were to introduce rational methods of agriculture . . . go in for cattle-breeding and so on . . . one could make a good living out of it. But they didn't do a thing, the swine. . . . He's probably a sot and a gambler—did you see his silly face?—and she's probably just interested in clothes, and extravagant. I know their sort!'

'How can you know them, Styopa?'

'I do! They complain they haven't anything to pay the interest with. How is it they can't find that two thousand, I'd like to know? If they were to introduce rational methods of agriculture, apply fertilisers to the soil and go in for cattle-breeding. . . . In general, if you consider the climatic and economic conditions, you could make a living out of just a couple of acres!'

Styopa went on chattering all the way home, and his wife listened to him and believed every word, but she did not recover her former mood. She could not get out of her head either Mikhailov's sour smile or the eyes filled with tears that for a moment had flashed at the window. When later the happy Styopa drove over twice to the auction and finally bought Mikhalkovo with the money of her dowry, she felt terribly uneasy. Her imagination kept conjuring up visions of Mikhailov and his family getting into the carriage and weeping as they left their beloved home. And the more gloomily and sentimentally her imagination worked, the more Styopa showed off. With the most obstinate self-assurance he discoursed on rational methods of agriculture, ordered a ton of books and magazines, ridiculed the Mikhailovs—and finally his agricultural dreams turned into the most shameless, audacious boasting. . . .

'You just see!' he said. 'I'm not Mikhailov, I'll show you how things should be run! Oh, yes!'

When the Kovalyovs moved into the deserted Mikhalkovo, the first things that caught Verochka's eye were the traces left by the previous inhabitants: a school time-table written in childish handwriting, a headless doll, a tomtit which flew in for crumbs, an inscription on a wall: 'Natasha is a fool', and so on. A great deal had to be repainted, repapered and pulled down before they could forget about other people's trouble.

A REPORTER'S DREAM

✻

'You are urgently requested to attend the French colony's ball to-day. I have no one else to send but you. Write a paragraph, with as much detail as possible. If, for any reason, you are unable to attend the ball, please inform me immediately. I shall ask someone else to go. Ticket enclosed herewith. Yours . . .' (followed by the editor's signature).

'P.S. There is to be a raffle. The prize will be a vase, which has been given by the President of the French Republic. I hope you'll win it.'

When he had read this letter Pyotr Semyonich, a reporter, lay down on the sofa, smoked a cigarette, and patted his chest and stomach with self-satisfaction. (He had just had dinner.)

'I hope you'll win it,' he mimicked the editor. 'And where shall I get the money from to buy a ticket? *He* won't give me any money for expenses, the swine. He's as stingy as Plyushkin. He ought to take example from the foreign papers. . . . They know how to value people. For instance, you, Stanley, are going to search for Livingstone? Fine. Take so many thousand pounds! You, John Bull, are going to search for "Jeanette"? Fine, take ten thousand! You're going to write up the French colony's ball? Fine. Take . . . about fifty thousand. . . . That's how they do it abroad! But he just sends me one ticket, and then he'll pay five copecks a line and he imagines . . . the swine!'

Pyotr Semyonich closed his eyes and was plunged in thought. A multitude of thoughts, great and small, crawled about in his head. But soon all these thoughts became covered with a sort of agreeable, pink mist. A jelly, semi-transparent and soft, began to ooze in every direction, from

172

every crevice, hole and window. . . . The ceiling began to sink. . . . Little men, little horses with ducks' heads ran about, some creature's large, soft wing waved, a river began to flow. . . . A little compositor went past carrying some very big letters, and smiled. . . . Then everything was drowned in his smile, and Pyotr Semyonich began to dream.

He put on a tail-coat and white gloves, and went out into the street. A carriage bearing the editor's monogram on it had been waiting for him at the entrance for a long time. A liveried footman leaped from the coachbox and helped him into the carriage, helped him into his seat just as if he were an aristocratic lady.

About a minute later the carriage stopped at the entrance of the Assembly Rooms. Frowning, he gave up his overcoat, and pompously went up a richly ornamented and illuminated staircase. (Terrific luxury.) Tropical plants, flowers from Nice, dresses costing thousands. . . .

'It's the correspondent . . .' a whisper ran through the crowd of many thousands of people. 'It is he. . . .'

A little old man with a solicitous expression and wearing decorations ran up to him.

'I beg your pardon!' he said to Pyotr Semyonich. 'Oh, I beg your pardon!'

'Oh, don't mention it! Really, you embarrass me . . .' said the reporter.

And suddenly, to his great amazement, he began to chatter in French. Before he had only known one word—'merci'—but now—just listen! Like that, with any luck, one could learn to speak Chinese.

Pyotr Semyonich took a flower and threw down a hundred roubles, and just at that moment a telegram from the editor was brought to him: 'Win the President of the French Republic's gift, and write your impressions. Reply paid for a thousand words. Don't worry about expense.' He went to the raffle and began to take tickets. He took one . . . two . . . ten. . . . Finally he took a hundred, a thousand, and received a Sèvres porcelain vase. Seizing the vase with both hands, he hurried on.

A little lady with luxurious flaxen hair and blue eyes came to meet him. Her dress was remarkable, above all criticism. A crowd followed her.

'Who is this?' the reporter asked.

'This is an illustrious Frenchwoman. She was ordered from Nice with the flowers. . . .'

Pyotr Semyonich went up to her and introduced himself. A moment later he took her arm, and walked on and on. . . . He had so many questions to ask the French girl, so many. . . . She was so delightful!

She's mine! he thought. But where shall I put the vase in my room? he wondered, admiring the French girl. His room was small, but the vase was growing and growing, and had grown so much that it would not even get into the room. He was on the point of tears.

'A-a-a . . . so you love the vase more than me, do you?' the French girl said to him suddenly, out of the blue; and bang! she hit the vase with her fist.

The valuable vessel cracked loudly and flew into pieces. The French girl laughed, and ran away somewhere into a mist, into a cloud. All the newspaper men stood round laughing. . . . Pyotr Semyonich, furious, foaming at the mouth, ran after them and suddenly, finding himself in the Bolshoi Theatre, fell head-downwards from the sixth tier.

Pyotr Semyonich opened his eyes, and saw that he was lying on the floor beside his own sofa. His bruised back and elbow ached.

Thank God there's no French girl! he thought, rubbing his eyes. So the vase isn't broken. It's a good thing I'm not married, if I were I dare say the children would start romping, and would break the vase.

But when he had rubbed his eyes thoroughly, of course he did not see the vase either.

It's all a dream, he thought. 'Still, it's one o'clock in the

morning already. The ball must have started ages ago . . .
it's time I went. . . . I'll just lie here a little bit longer, and
then—off I go!'

But when he had lain there a little bit longer he stretched
and . . . fell asleep—and so he never got to the French
colony's ball.

'Well?' the editor asked him next day. 'Did you go to the
ball? Did you enjoy it?'

'So-so. . . . Nothing special,' he said, making a bored
face. 'Tame. Dull. I wrote it up in two hundred lines. I
scolded our society a bit for not knowing how to have a
good time.' When he had said this he turned towards the
window and thought of the editor:

'The s-w-i-n-e!!'

ONE MAN'S MEAT

※

IT was after two o'clock in the morning. The Fibrovs, husband and wife, were not asleep. He was tossing from side to side, constantly spitting, while she—a small, thin brunette —was lying motionless and looking thoughtfully at the open window, through which peeped the dour and unsociable dawn. . . .

'I can't sleep!' she sighed. 'Do you feel sick?'

'Yes, a bit.'

'I can't understand, Vasya, why you aren't fed up with coming home every day in such a state! There's not a single night without you feeling ill. You ought to be ashamed of yourself!'

'Well, I'm sorry. . . . I don't do it on purpose. I drank a bottle of beer at the editor's office, then I had a drop more at the "Arkadia". Forgive me.'

'Oh, what is there to forgive? You ought to think it repulsive and disgusting yourself. Spitting, hiccoughing. . . . You look like nothing on earth. Why, it's every night, every night! I can't remember when you came home sober.'

'I don't want to drink, but somehow it just goes down of its own accord. It's such a damn awful job—you rush about town all day. You have a glass of vodka somewhere, beer somewhere else, and in yet another place you meet a friend who's having a drink, you see . . . it's impossible not to drink. Another time you can't get any information without splitting a bottle of vodka with some swine or other. For example, today at that fire I couldn't very well not have a drink with the agent.'

'Yes, it's an awful job!' the brunette sighed. 'You should give it up, Vasya!'

'Give it up? How can I!'

'Of course you can. It would be all right if you were a real writer, if you wrote good poetry or stories, but as it is you're just a reporter, writing about thefts and fires. You write such nonsense—makes one ashamed to read it sometimes. It wouldn't be so bad if you earned a lot, two or three hundred roubles a month say, but you get a miserable fifty roubles, and even that's not regular. The flat's poor and dirty, and it stinks of laundry, and we're surrounded by workmen and loose women. You hear nothing but vulgar words and songs all day. We haven't any furniture or linen. You're miserably dressed, like a pauper, so that the landlady calls you by your Christian name, while I'm worse than any milliner. We don't eat half as well as workmen. . . . You eat some mess or other, somewhere in town, in pubs, and you probably don't even pay for that yourself, I. . . . God alone knows what I eat! If we were working class, uneducated, then I'd be reconciled to this existence, but after all you're from a good family, went to the university, you speak French. I went to a good school, I'm used to being pampered.'

'You wait, Katyusha, they'll ask me to run the gossip column in the *Night-Blindness*—then we'll live differently. I'll take a flat then.'

'You've been promising me that for three years now. And what's the point anyway, even if they do ask you? However much you get you'll just drink it all away. It isn't as if you'd give up going about with your writers and actors! But d'you know what, Vasya? I ought to write to my uncle Dmitri Fedorich in Tula. He'd find you a splendid job somewhere in a bank or a government office. It would be fine, Vasya! You'd go to the office like other people, on the twentieth of every month you'd get your salary—and no worry! We'd rent a detached house with its own yard and sheds and a hayloft. You can rent a splendid house there for two hundred

a year. We'd buy furniture, china, table-cloths, we'd have a
cook and have dinner every day. You'd come back from the
office at three, glance at the table, and it would be laid ever
so neat, and there'd be radishes and all sorts of different
kinds of snacks. We'd get chickens, ducks, pigeons, we'd buy
a cow. In the provinces, if you don't live luxuriously and
drink your money away, you could have all that on a
thousand roubles a year. And our children wouldn't die of
damp, like they do now, and I wouldn't have to drag myself
to the hospital all the time. Vasya, I beg you, for Heaven's
sake let's go and live in the provinces.'

'I'd die of boredom with the savages there.'

'Well, is it so gay here? We've no social life, we don't
know anyone. . . . Clean or fairly decent people you
only have a business acquaintanceship with, but you don't
know anyone's family. Who comes to see us? Well, who?
That Cleopatra Sergeyevna. . . . You think she's a celebrity,
she writes musical feuilletons, but I think—she's a kept
woman, a loose woman. Well, how can a woman drink
vodka and take her corsets off with men looking on? She
writes articles, talks about honesty all the time, but she
borrowed a rouble from me last year, and hasn't paid it
back to this day. Then there's that beloved poet of yours
that comes to see you. You pride yourself on knowing such
a famous man, but tell me honestly, is he worth it?'

'You couldn't have an honester man!'

'But he isn't much fun. He only comes here to get drunk.
He drinks and tells smutty stories. The day before yesterday,
for example, he got sozzled and slept the whole night here
on the floor. And the actors! When I was a girl I worshipped
those celebrities, but since I married you it riles me just to
look at a theatre. They're always drunk and coarse, they
don't know how to behave in female company, they're
supercilious, they go about in dirty jack-boots. Terribly
trying people! I can't understand what you find funny in
those stories of theirs, which they tell with loud, raucous

laughter! And you look at them somehow ingratiatingly, just as if those celebrities were doing you a favour by knowing you. . . . Ugh!'

'Oh stop it, please!'

'But there, in the provinces, civil servants would come to see us, school teachers, officers. Educated, gentle people they all are, without pretensions. They'd have a cup of tea, and a glass of vodka if they were offered it, and go home. No noise, no stories, it would be dignified like that, considerate. You know, they'd be sitting in armchairs and on the sofa, discussing all sorts of things, and then the maid would hand tea round, with jam and biscuits. After tea they'd play the piano, sing, dance. It would be so nice, Vasya! At about midnight there'd be a light snack: sausage, cheese, the roast left over from dinner. After supper you'd see the ladies to their homes, and I'd stay at home and tidy up.'

'It would be boring, Katyusha!'

'If it was boring at home, then you could go to the club, or for a walk. . . . If you go for a walk here you don't meet a soul you know, you take to drink willy-nilly, but there you'd know everyone you met. You could talk to whoever you felt like talking to . . . teachers, lawyers, doctors— there'd be plenty of people to say an intelligent word to. They take a great interest in educated people there, Vasya! You'd be one of the leading lights there.'

And Katyusha went on dreaming aloud for a long time. The lead-grey light outside the window gradually changed to white. . . . The silence of night yielded its place imperceptibly to the bustle of morning. The reporter was not asleep, but listening and constantly raising his heavy head to spit. Suddenly, when Katyusha was least expecting it, he sat up sharply and leaped out of bed. . . . His face was pale, there was sweat on his forehead. . . .

'I feel deuced sick,' he interrupted Katyusha's dreaming. 'Wait a moment, I'm just coming. . . .'

He covered his shoulders with a blanket, and ran quickly

out of the room. He was a victim to that unpleasant occurrence which is so well-known to drunkards in the morning. About two minutes later he returned, pale and languid. . . . His walk was unsteady. . . . His face bore an expression of disgust, of despair, almost of terror, as if he had only just understood all the outward unsightliness of his way of life. The daylight lit up all the poverty and dirt of his room for him, and the expression of hopelessness on his face became more acute.

'Katyusha, write to your uncle!' he muttered.

'Really? You agree?' exclaimed the brunette in triumph. 'I'll write to-morrow, and I give you my word of honour that you'll get a splendid job! Vasya, you . . . you are being serious?'

'Please, Katyusha, do . . . for God's sake.'

And Katyusha once more began to dream aloud. Lulled by the sound of her own voice, she soon fell asleep. She dreamed of a detached house, of a farmyard in which her own ducks and hens were sedately pacing. She saw pigeons looking at her from a dormer window, and heard the cow mooing. Around all was quiet; there were no fellow lodgers, no raucous laughter, not even the hateful, hurried squeak of pens could be heard. Vasya, a picture of dignity and decorum, was striding through the front garden to the gate. He was going to the office. And her heart was filled with that feeling of peace which is undisturbed by desire and thought. . . .

At mid-day she woke up in a capital frame of mind. Sleep had had a salutary effect on her. But then she rubbed her eyes and looked at the place where, not long ago, Vasya had been tossing and turning, and the joy which had seized her fell away from her like a piece of lead. Vasya was gone, to came back late at night drunk, as he had come back yesterday, the day before . . . always. . . . Again she would day dream, again a look of disgust would flash across his face.

'There's no point in writing to uncle!' she sighed.

THE GUEST

(*A Scene*)

❉

ZELTERSKI, a solicitor, could not keep his eyes open. Nature
was plunged in darkness. "The breeze had fallen, the choirs
of birds were silent, and the herds were lying down." Zelterski's wife had gone to bed long ago, the servants were
sleeping too, all the livestock was asleep, only Zelterski
himself could not go to his bedroom, although his eyelids
weighed a ton. The fact was that he had a guest, a retired
colonel called Peregarin, who lived in a neighbouring country
villa. He had arrived after dinner, had sat down on the sofa,
and had not once moved since then, just as if he was stuck
to it. He was sitting there and recounting in a hoarse, nasal
voice how he had been bitten by a mad dog in Kremenchug
in 1842. He finished telling the story, and then began it
from the beginning all over again. Zelterski was in despair.
He would have done anything to get rid of his guest! He
frequently looked at his watch, said that his head ached,
and often left the room where his guest was sitting—but it
was all of no avail. His guest did not understand, and went
on talking about the mad dog.

Zelterski was furious. The old fool will sit here till morning! he thought. What a blockhead! Well, if he doesn't
understand ordinary hints, stronger measures will have to
be taken. 'Listen,' he said aloud. 'Do you know what I like
about country life?'

'What?'

'The fact that one can lead a regular life here. In town
it's difficult to keep to a regular régime, whereas here it's
just the opposite. We get up at nine, dine at three, have

supper at ten, and by midnight we're asleep. I'm always in bed by twelve. Heaven forbid that I should go to bed later. I can't get rid of my migraine the next day if I do!'

'You don't say! Of course, it depends on what you're used to. You know, I used to have a friend called Klyushkin, a captain. I got to know him in Serpukhovo. Well now, this Klyushkin. . . .'

And the colonel, hiccoughing, smacking his lips, and gesticulating with plump fingers, began to tell him about Klyushkin. It had already struck midnight, the hand of the clock was reaching towards half-past twelve, but he still went on telling his story. Zelterski was thrown into a sweat.

He doesn't understand! The silly ass! he thought, irritated. Does he really think that his visit gives me pleasure? Now, how can I get rid of him? 'Listen,' he interrupted the colonel. 'What should I do? My throat hurts terribly! I don't know what the hell possessed me this morning—I went to see a friend whose child is ill with diphtheria. I've probably caught it. Yes, I feel I've caught it. I've got diphtheria!'

'It does happen!' said Peregarin imperturbably, in a nasal voice.

'It's a dangerous illness! It's not only that I'm ill myself, but I can give it to other people too. The illness is infectious to the highest degree. I only hope that I won't give it to you, Parfeni Savvich!'

'To me? Ha-ha! I've lived in fever hospitals and didn't catch anything—and you think I'll catch it from you! ha-ha. . . . No, old chap, an old fogey like me won't catch any illnesses. Old men are tough. We had a little old man in our brigade, a Colonel Trébien. . . . He was of French origin. Well now, this Trébien. . . .'

And Peregarin began to describe how tough Trébien had been. The clock struck half-past twelve.

'Forgive me for interrupting you, Parfeni Savvich,' groaned Zelterski. 'At what time do you go to bed?'

'Sometimes at two, sometimes at three, and sometimes I don't go to bed at all, especially if I'm in good company, or if my rheumatism's bothering me. To-day, for example, I shall go to bed at about four, because I had a good sleep before dinner. I can do without sleep altogether. During the war we sometimes didn't go to bed for weeks on end. I remember once, we were stationed near Akhaltsykh. . . .'

'Excuse me, but I always go to bed at twelve. I get up at nine, so I have to go to bed early, willy-nilly.'

'Of course. It's good for the health, too, to get up early. Well, it was like this . . . we were stationed near Akhaltsykh. . . .'

'It's the very devil. . . . I feel shivery, feverish. It's always like that with me before one of my fits. I should tell you that I sometimes have strange, nervous fits. At about one o'clock in the morning . . . the fits never occur in the day-time . . . suddenly a noise starts in my head: buzz-buzz-buzz. . . . I lose my senses, leap up and start throwing whatever household utensils there may be lying about. If there's a knife near—I throw the knife, if there's a chair—I throw that. I feel shivery now, it's probably a fit coming on. It always begins with shivering.'

'Did you ever! You should have treatment for it!'

'I've had treatment, it doesn't help. . . . I just confine myself to warning my friends and the household that they should go away shortly before a fit, but I've given up having treatment ages ago.'

'Pss. . . . What illnesses one does come across in this world! Plague, and cholera, and all sorts of fits. . . .'

The colonel shook his head and was plunged in thought. Silence fell.

How would it be if I read him my book? the thought occurred to Zelterski. I've got that novel of mine lying about somewhere, I wrote it when I was still at school. . . . It might be of service now. . . . 'Oh, by the way,' Zelterski interrupted Peregarin's reflections, 'wouldn't you like me to read you something I've written? I concocted something in my leisure hours. A novel in five parts, with a prologue and epilogue.'

And, without waiting for an answer, Zelterski jumped up and fished out from the drawer of his table an old, yellow manuscript, on which was written in large letters: 'The Swell: A Novel in Five Parts.'

Now he'll surely go away, mused Zelterski, turning over the pages of his youthful peccadillo. I'll go on reading to him till he howls. . . . 'Well, now listen, Parfeni Savvich. . . .'

'With pleasure. . . . I like it. . . .'

Zelterski began to read. The colonel crossed his legs, settled himself more comfortably, and made a serious face, evidently preparing himself to listen conscientiously and for a long time. The reader began with a description of nature. When the clock struck one nature yielded its place to a description of the castle in which lived the hero of the novel, Count Valentin Blenski.

'I'd like to live in a castle like that!' sighed Peregarin. 'And it's so well written! I could sit and listen to it for ages!'

You wait a bit! thought Zelterski. You'll howl soon!

At half-past one the castle gave way to a description of the hero's handsome personal appearance. . . . Precisely at two o'clock the reader read in a quiet, subdued voice:

' "You ask, what do I desire? Oh, I desire that there, far away, beneath the vaults of the southern sky, your little hand should languidly tremble in my hand. . . . There, only there, will my heart throb stronger beneath the vaults of my spiritual edifice. . . . Love, love!" No, Parfeni Savvich. . . . I can't go on. . . . I'm at the end of my tether!'

'Well, drop it. You'll finish it to-morrow, but let's talk now. . . . Well now, I haven't told you yet what happened at Akhaltsykh. . . .'

Zelterski, worn out, threw himself back in the sofa and, closing his eyes, began to listen. . . .

I've tried everything, he thought. Not a single bullet has pierced this mammoth hide. Now he'll sit here till four o'clock. . . . Lord, I'd give a hundred roubles now to flop into bed this very instant. . . . Ah! Let's ask him for a loan! That's an excellent method. . . . 'Parfeni Savvich,' he interrupted the colonel. 'I'm interrupting you again. I want to ask you a little favour. . . . The fact is that lately, living here in the country, I've been spending an awful lot. I simply haven't got a penny, but I'm expecting some money at the end of August.'

'But. . . . I've stayed too long . . .' snorted Peregarin, looking round for his cap. 'It's after two already. . . . What's that you were saying?'

'I'd like to borrow two or three hundred roubles from someone. . . . You don't know anyone who could lend me that?'

'How should I? Still . . . it's time you went to bye-byes. . . . Good-bye. . . . Remember me to your wife. . . .'

The colonel took his cap and made a step towards the door.

'Where are you off to?' said Zelterski in triumph. 'And I wanted to ask you. . . . Knowing your kindness, I hoped. . . .'

'To-morrow, but now—off to my wife—quick march! She's probably been waiting up for her loved one. . . . Ha-ha-ha! Good-bye, my dear fellow. . . . Off to bed!'

Peregarin pressed Zelterski's hand quickly, put on his cap, and went out. His host was triumphant.

HISTORICAL NOTES

THE WOMAN IN THE CASE (*Roman s Kontrabasom*)
Russian title: *Romance with a Double Bass*. First printed in the periodical *Oskolki*, 1886, under the pseudonym A. Chekhonte. Reprinted, with a few slight changes, in the Collected Works, 1899.

A VISIT TO FRIENDS (*U Znakomykh*)
First published in the *Cosmopolis* (Russian section), Vol. IX, No. 2, February, 1898. Reprinted in an anthology *A Memorial to A. P. Chekhov. Poetry and Prose*, published in St. Petersburg, 1906.

APPROPRIATE MEASURES (*Nadlejashchie Mery*)
First published in the journal *Oskolki*, 22 September, 1884, with the sub-title: (*A scene*). Signed: A. Chekhonte. Included in the anthology *Pyostrye Rasskazy* (*Motley Stories*), St. Petersburg, 1886. Included, in a slightly changed version, in the Collected Works, 1899. The translation is made from the revised text.

THE BOA-CONSTRICTOR AND THE RABBIT (*Udav i Krolik*)
First published in the *Peterburgskaya Gazeta*, 20 April, 1887. Signed: A. Chekhonte. The story is based on a story written in 1886, which was forbidden by the censor: *For the Information of Husbands*.

HISTORY OF A BUSINESS ENTERPRISE (*Istoriya Odnogo Torgovovo Predpriyatiya*)
First published in the magazine *Oskolki*, 2 May, 1892, under the pseudonym 'Grach' ('The rook').

75,000
First published in the magazine *Budilnik*, 13 January, 1884. Signed: A. Chekhonte.

THE MASK (*Maska*)
First published in the magazine *Razvlechenie*, 27 October, 1884, with the title: *Noli me tangere* (*From the life of a Provincial Ace*). Signed: A. Chekhonte. Included, in a greatly revised version, in the Collected Works, 1900. The translation is made from the revised text.

AN UNPLEASANT INCIDENT (*Nepriyatnost*)
First published in *Novoye Vremya*, 3 and 7 June, 1888. Title: *A Worrying Trifle*. Signed: An. Chekhov. Included, with new title and some changes, in the anthology: *Gloomy People*, St. Petersburg, 1890 (and nine subsequent editions, St. Petersburg, 1891–99). Included, with some changes and omissions, in the Collected Works, 1901. The translation is made from the text of 1901.

THE EVE OF THE TRIAL (*Noch pered Sudom*)
First published in the magazine *Oskolki*, 1 Feb., 1886. Subtitle: (*A case from my Practice as a Quack Doctor*). Signed: A. Chekhonte. Published, with slight changes, in an anthology *Innocent Speech* (*Nevinnye Rechi*), Moscow, 1887. Included, with further changes, in the Collected Works, 1889. The translation is made from the text of 1889. The story was written in 1884, when Chekhov sent it to the magazine *Strekoza* (*The Dragonfly*), but the manuscript was mislaid by the editors. Later on, Chekhov thought of turning the story into a farce, and some notes for it are preserved in Moscow.

SINISTER NIGHT (*Nedobraya Noch*)
First printed in the *Peterburgskaya Gazeta*, 3 November, 1886. Signed: A. Chekhonte.

THE LODGER (*Jilets*)
First printed in the journal *Oskolki*, 1 November, 1886, where it was called *The Lodger in No. 31*. Reprinted with considerable changes in *Journal dlya vsekh*, No. 11, 1898. The translation has been made from the revised text.

THE DREAM (A CHRISTMAS STORY) (*Son* (*Svyatochny Rasskaz*))
First published in the *Peterburgskaya Gazeta*, 25 December, 1885. Signed: A. Chekhonte. The story was written sometime in 1884.

OUT OF SHEER BOREDOM (*Ot nechevo delat*)
First printed 26 May, 1886, in the *Peterburgskaya Gazeta*. Signed: A. Chekhonte.

A DISAGREEABLE EXPERIENCE (*Nepriyatnaya Istoriya*)
First published in the *Peterburgskaya Gazeta*, 29 June, 1887. Signed: A. Chekhonte.

HIS FIRST APPEARANCE (*Pervy Debyut*)
First published in the *Peterburgskaya Gazeta*, 13 January, 1886. Signed: A. Chekhonte.

HOLY SIMPLICITY (*Svyataya Prostota*)
First published in the *Peterburgskaya Gazeta*, 9 December, 1885.
Signed: A. Chekhonte.

THE DIPLOMAT (*Diplomat*)
First published in the *Peterburgskaya Gazeta*, 20 May, 1885.
Signed: A. Chekhonte.

MUTUAL SUPERIORITY (*Oba Luchshe*) (*Both are Better*)
First published in the magazine *Oskolki*, 30 March, 1885. Sub-
title: *A Story*. Signed: A. Chekhonte. Included, without a subtitle
and with a few slight changes, in the anthology: *Pyostrye Rasskazy*
(*Motley Stories*), St. Petersburg, 1886. The translation is made
from the revised text.

TAEDIUM VITAE (*Skuka Jizni*)
First printed in *Novoye Vremya*, 31 May, 1886. Signed: An.
Chekhov.

OTHER PEOPLE'S TROUBLE (*Chujaya Beda*)
First printed in *Peterburgskaya Gazeta*, 28 July, 1886. Signed: A.
Chekhonte.

A REPORTER'S DREAM (*Son Reportera*)
First published in the magazine *Budilnik*, 18 February, 1884.
Title: *The French Ball: A Dream Fantasy*. Signed: A. Chekhonte.
Chekhov originally intended to include this story in the Collected
Works, 1899, and he revised the story for this edition and changed
the title. In the original version there were references to Moscow
journalists and writers, but in the revised version Chekhov
omitted personal remarks and proper names. The translation
is made from the text (the galley-proof) of the revised version.
The ball described in the story took place on 17 February, 1884.

ONE MAN'S MEAT . . . (*Kon i Trepetnaya Lan*) (*The Horse and
the Tremulous Doe*).
Signed: A. Chekhonte. First published in the *Peterburgskaya
Gazeta*, 12 August, 1885. Sub-title: *A Scene*. Reprinted, with
no subtitle and some changes, in the anthology *Pyostrye Rasskazy*
(*Motley Stories*), St. Petersburg, 1886. The translation is made
from the text of 1886.

THE GUEST (*Gost*)
First published in the *Peterburgskaya Gazeta*, 5 August, 1885.
Signed: A. Chekhonte.